ALL—OR NOTHING

Lionel Eden was furious when he saw Catherine return from her tête-à-tête with the elegant and infamous Earl of Deeds.

Lionel seized her arm and led her to a small antechamber, and shut the door behind them.

"Whatever are you doing, sir?" Catherine asked. "It is not at all the thing for us to be private like this."

"Did you object to being private with Lord Deeds?" Lionel demanded. "He is not for you. He will only ruin you."

"What right do you have to tell me this?" Catherine retorted. "What I do, whom I see, is none of your concern. Not now. Not anymore. Not since you declared your engagement to Mary Gardner."

She saw Lionel's cheekbones redden, and she felt a stab of triumph. "But since you are so interested in my affairs, I will tell you that I am contemplating marriage to the earl."

This was Catherine's ultimate gamble to win Lionel at last. But what a price she would have to pay if she lost. . . .

(For a list of other Signet Regency Romances by Barbara Hazard, please turn page.)

A Signet Super Regency

"A tender and sensitive love story . . . an exciting blend of romance and history"
—*Romantic Times*

The Guarded Heart

Barbara Hazard

*Passion and danger embraced her—
but one man intoxicated her flesh
with love's irresistable promise . . .*

Beautiful Erica Stone found her husband mysteriously murdered in Vienna and herself alone and helpless in this city of romance . . . until the handsome, cynical Owen Kingsley, Duke of Graves, promised her protection if she would spy for England among the licentious lords of Europe. Aside from the danger and intrigue, Erica found herself wrestling with her passion, for the tantalizingly reserved Duke, when their first achingly tender kiss sparked a desire in her more powerfully exciting than her hesitant heart had ever felt before. . . .

Lady Lochinvar

Barbara Hazard

A SIGNET BOOK

NEW AMERICAN LIBRARY

SIGNET TRADEMARK REG. U.S.PAT. OFF. AND FOREIGN COUNTRIES
REGISTERED TRADEMARK—MARCA REGISTRADA
HECHO EN CHICAGO, U.S.A.

SIGNET, SIGNET CLASSIC, MENTOR, ONYX, PLUME, MERIDIAN and
NAL BOOKS are published by NAL PENGUIN, INC.,
1633 Broadway, New York, New York 10019

First Printing, November, 1987

1 2 3 4 5 6 7 8 9

PRINTED IN THE UNITED STATES OF AMERICA

*This book is for Kay and Joe,
and for Jerry and Alex.*

O, young Lochinvar is come out of the west,
Through all the wide border, his steed was the best.
And save his good broadsword, he weapons had none;
He rode all unarmed, and he rode all alone.
So faithful in love, and so dauntless in war,
There never was knight like the young Lochinvar.

—Sir Walter Scott
from *Marmion*, Canto V

One

LADY CATHERINE CAHILL fell in love for the first and only time in her life at precisely three thirty-five in the afternoon on the fourteenth of December, eighteen hundred and eleven.

She had just arrived at the Duke and Duchess of Wynne's principal seat, in company with her parents, and her brother and sister. Her father, Reginald Cahill, Marquess of Deane, was a cousin of the duke's and, as had become customary, had brought his family to visit at Christmastime. The duke and duchess held open house at that time every year for those members of the family, no matter how distantly related they might be, who could attend. Their hospitality was warm and genuine, and a large group generally assembled to spend at least three happy weeks together. There was plenty of room, after all, for Wynne was a huge stone palace set in a spacious park and surrounded by hundred of acres in the heart of Buckinghamshire.

Lady Catherine had just stepped down from the lead traveling carriage. She began to walk up and down somewhat impatiently while her mother gave the footmen orders about the baggage, and her sister warned her maid to take special care of the bandbox that contained her new bonnet. Since the marquess and his son were deep in conversation with the elderly butler, who had come out to greet them, Lady Catherine was the only member of the family who was not occupied.

She looked around, admiring Wynne and its park anew. As she did so, a trio of riders came galloping up the drive. It was obvious they were racing each other, for their cries to their mounts were clearly audible in the cold, crisp air. The lady's eye was caught by the leader's horse, a large chestnut gelding with powerful hindquarters and a noble head.

Almost as an afterthought, she inspected the rider as he came abreast of the carriages and reined in, laughing in triumph and waving his hat to his defeated companions. The low winter sun lit his thick auburn hair with brilliant highlights, and the color the exercise in the cold December afternoon had brought to his handsome, masculine face made him seem larger than life; vibrant, almost godlike. Suddenly, beside her, her brother Emery exclaimed, and he hurried forward to shake the rider's hand.

Lady Catherine's green eyes with their distinctive gold flecks widened as she felt a little stir deep inside. She did not know what that stirring meant, for although Cupid's darts are invariably swift and unfailing accurate, they cause no pain when they find their mark. And, of course, she had never been honored by the merry little cherub before.

"I say, Summers, isn't that one of the Marquess of Sutherland's brood?" she heard her father ask in his deep loud bass.

Lady Catherine did not take her eyes from the handsome young man before her; indeed, she found it impossible to do so.

As the white-haired butler gave an assent, Lord Deane turned to his wife. "I don't think we've seen the young scamp for several years, have we, Rose?"

The gentleman under discussion patted the gelding's neck before giving him into a groom's care. As he strolled nearer, accompanied by her brother and his two companions, Lady Catherine saw dark blue eyes under a pair of straight brows, eyes that sparkled with smiling good humor. The dart twisted deeper into her heart.

"Give you good day, sir!" he said to the marquess as he bowed. "But I must object to being called a young scamp now, m'lord," he added, his smile white and wide in his glowing face. "You are remembering the occasion five years ago when my cousins and I caused a bit of a stir here by hiding all the Christmas gifts in the North Tower, are you not?"

"A bit of a stir, was it?" the marquess asked, chuckling in memory. "It was more than that, young Eden!"

"Ah, but much must be forgiven a high-spirited youth of only fifteen summers, isn't that so, Aunt Rose?" He bowed again before he kissed Lady Deane's cheek and hugged her.

"No doubt you are right, Lionel," the marchioness said with a sigh. "My own son seems to have been cut from the same yard of cloth. Perhaps it runs in the family?"

The two young men exchanged glances and laughed in unison.

Lady Catherine stood very still when the viscount greeted her sister Millicent next. She saw how Millie blushed, and how she fluttered her eyelashes at all the young men, for all the world as if she had a giant cinder in both eyes, Lady Catherine thought scornfully. But she was not at all pleased when she observed the keen interest with which Lionel Eden, Viscount Benning, admired her pretty sister, and she moved closer to her father to tug his sleeve.

"And this, of course, is Kitty," he said. "I daresay you don't remember her."

"Of course I do," the viscount said gallantly as he bowed.

Lady Catherine saw her brother's smile, and heard her sister's titter, and she put up her chin. "Lady

Catherine," she corrected her father. He looked amazed, and now everyone was smiling.

"I shall have to present George and Harry to you by their titles, so formal as you have become," the viscount teased her. "And why should that be, when we all remember the big-eyed child I used to call Miss Kitty-cat?"

"I have grown up since then, m'lord," Lady Catherine managed to say, very much aware of her heightened color and the way her heart was beating so erratically at her joy that he did indeed remember her.

"Do let us go in," the marchioness suggested, beckoning to them all. "It is such a raw day!"

Lady Catherine saw the viscount hesitate, but then that same heart leapt as he offered her his arm. "May I, m'lady?" he asked, his dark blue eyes twinkling down at her. As she nodded and took his arm, she saw him holding out his other arm to her sister, and all the happiness she had felt to be singled out by him disappeared in a flash of jealousy. Behind her, she heard George Benson mutter to his brother Harry, "If that isn't just like Lion, to snabble all the ladies for himself!"

"Of any age," Lord Benson agreed wryly.

Lady Catherine could not think of a single thing to say, although on the viscount's other side her sister prattled on easily about their journey and some family news. Since Lady Catherine had never been at all shy, she found this unusual reticence very strange.

The group stepped into the high-ceilinged hall of Wynne to be greeted not only by a smiling duchess, but by three of the sheep dogs she bred as well. Excited by the new company, they wagged their tails and barked, jumping up on each guest as if to ensure they had a proper welcome. Lady Catherine's lip curled in scorn as her sister cringed against the viscount, making shooing motions to keep the dogs away from her blue velvet cloak.

"Enough, my pets, enough!" the duchess scolded as she beckoned to a footman. "Take them away, Gerston," she said. "It is impossible to even say hello in all this noisy confusion."

As the footman obeyed, she turned to her newest guests. "Dear Rose, Reginald, how good to see you again, and your family, too. Why, how pretty you have grown, Millicent!" she added, clapping her hands a little.

Lady Catherine waited, but the duchess only smiled at her and her brother before she led the way to the drawing room. "I ordered tea for you the moment I learned of your arrival," she said, taking Lady Deane's cloak and bonnet. "Do come nearer the fire, Rose, you must be chilled through. Such a long drive from Devon, is it not?

"May we join you, too, duchess?" the viscount asked. "We are just as cold after our ride."

"But of course, Lionel," the duchess agreed. She was a tall, middleaged woman with a pleasant face. As a girl she had been admired for her tiny waist and supple figure, although she had never had any delusions about her beauty. Now, serene and happy in her marriage, she was completely unconcerned that that famous waist had deserted her forever after the birth of her fourth child.

The viscount led the ladies he was escorting to a sofa, and went to fetch them some tea. In his absence, his cousin Harry was quick to come over and talk to Lady Millicent. Harry and George Benson were older than the viscount, and Lady Catherine did not think them nearly as good-looking, although she could see the strong family resemblance. She wondered why this was so, as her eyes returned to the viscount's broad-shouldered back as he bent to accept the cups the duchess handed him. She watched him as he made his way back to the sofa, not hearing a word Lord Benson was saying to her sister, nor her replies.

As she took the cup he offered, the viscount grinned

at her. "You may have grown up, Lady Catherine, but your eyes are just the same," he told her. "Just like a cat's, so wide and unblinking."

Lady Catherine longed to ask him if he admired cats, as he added, "Of course, I much prefer dogs, as most men do, I think. Not that cats don't have their uses, mind you."

"Does your father keep that pack of hounds still?" Lord Deane asked curiously. "Never knew a man so intent on his hunting dogs as Roy Eden!"

"Indeed he does, sir," the viscount said, turning away from the ladies a little to reply.

"I am very fond of dogs," Lady Catherine interrupted, determined to keep the viscount's attention at all costs. She had removed her warm pelisse and bonnet, and, somewhat irrelevantly, she wished she had not worn her old merino gown for traveling. And when she remembered how she had scorned Millie's concern for her attire this morning, she had to shake her head. How much better it would have been if she were dressed in the new green velvet!

"Are you, Miss Kittycat?" the viscount asked idly. "And you, Lady Millicent, do you like dogs, too?"

When her sister hesitated, Lady Catherine said, "No, she does not. Why, if father kept dogs, I don't know what she'd do. Faint a lot, I suppose. She's always been afraid of them, haven't you, Millie?"

Lady Millicent blushed, and lowered her eyes to stare into her cup of tea. "I am sure they are very nice," she said in her soft voice. Both young gentlemen leaned closer to hear her. "It is just that I am not accustomed to them."

Lady Catherine saw the viscount's expressive eyes brighten, and she would have continued to bemoan her sister's timidity for the entire animal kingdom, most especially toads, snakes, and spiders, except she caught her mother's warning eye and subsided.

A footman presented a plate of cakes then, and Lord

Deane engaged the young men in a private conversation.

"Whatever is the matter with you, Kitty?" Lady Millicent asked from behind her napkin. "I have never seen even you so forward, so rude! Take care or Mama will be banishing you without delay. You know how she hates bad manners!"

Lady Catherine was not required to answer, for the duchess beckoned her to her side just then, and she was forced to go and chat with her hostess and her mama. But throughout teatime, her eyes rarely left the viscount for long. She was sure he was the best-looking man she had ever seen, but his appeal was more than that. True, he was tall, with an athletic build, and he had a strong jaw and regular features which taken separately or as a whole could not be faulted. But it was the light in his eyes, the wit and good humor, and the kindness she fancied she saw lurking there that attracted her. And she knew she was not mistaken in him, for she remembered other Christmas visits in years past when he had always taken time to be kind, and to speak to her. Why, once he had even scolded her nemesis, that horrid Garth Allendon, for teasing her and pulling her braids.

Now she watched him as he put his head back and laughed at something her father was saying, a lock of his thick auburn hair falling over his forehead as he did so. Lady Catherine put her teacup down carefully and clasped her hands together in her lap as she felt that little stirring deep inside again.

It seemed much too short a time before her mother rose and said, "Come, girls. We must go up and oversee the unpacking now, as well as change for dinner."

The duchess rose as well, and smiled. "I have put you and your daughters in the west wing, my dear. Emery, of course, joins the other young men in the bachelor's wing. Summers will show you to your rooms and see that you are settled. We dine at six, for we still keep country hours here. The children will have their dinner in the gold salon as usual, excepting those who eat in the nursery. We have quite a crowd of babies this year. Doris brought her twins, and did you hear about Donald and Mary's newest addition? I cannot wait for you to see him, he is the dearest baby!''

As the duchess walked with her guests to the door of the drawing room, she continued to tell Lady Deane about the guests who had arrived before her, and those who were still expected. Lady Catherine did not hear a word. She was wondering rather desperately if there was any chance she might convince her mother that she was old enough to join the grownups this year in Wynne's impressive scarlet and gold dining salon. She knew very well there was not, and her heart plummeted. The magic age for that rite of passage had always been sixteen, and since she would not even have her thirteenth birthday until May, she was far from being considered eligible. Her gold-flecked eyes smoldered with disappointment, and her lower lip came out in a distinct pout, making her look not only sullen, but very young as well.

Viscount Benning did not notice, for he was deep in a discussion with her brother Emery. Although Emery Cahill was, at nineteen, a year his junior, they had always been friendly, although they did not see each other except at family gatherings like this. And Lord Benning had been absent from the group for the past two years. He had spent those years in the West Indies with his aunt and uncle, who had an extensive sugar cane plantation and mill operation there. Lord Sutherland had decided that learning the plantation business would be an excellent opportunity for his youngest son, for there were three brothers between him and the title, and his own brother and sister-in-law were childless.

The tea party separated in the huge hall, the Cahills to retire to their rooms, and the young men to adjourn to the billiard room for a game or two before it was time to dress for dinner.

Lord Benning bowed over both Lady Millicent's and Lady Catherine's hands. His eyes twinkled as he told them how delighted he was that they had arrived, and how much he was looking forward to renewing their acquaintance.

As the two ladies followed the duchess's elderly butler up the impressive, wide staircase, Lady Catherine heard her mother murmur behind her, "What a surprise to find Lionel so mature and polished, is it not, my dear? His years in the West Indies have served him well. Why, when I remember the pranks he played as a boy, the way he was never still, I am amazed!"

"He is not all that mature, Rose," her father replied. "And under that veneer of polish is a very eager young man, up to every rig and row in town. Didn't you see how taken he was with Millie? Best you keep an eye on him, and your daughter, too, ma'am. Lionel Eden's a handsome young devil, and the mischief he might get into now, given the slightest opportunity, is something I am sure neither of us would care to contemplate."

Lady Catherine was sure her sister had not heard a word of her father's lecture, for she was busy whispering about the gown she planned to wear to dinner, and hoping her maid had not only unpacked the deep blue muslin, but pressed it as well. Lady Catherine's pout grew more pronounced. Being only twelve, she did not have a maid, and any attention her own gown needed would have to wait until a housemaid could attend to it.

As she marched down the long hallway to the west wing, she conceded that it hardly mattered what she wore, or how it looked. She would have little chance to see the viscount again this evening. True, she might be summoned with the other children after dinner, but she would be banished with them as well, after only a little while in company. The duchess had firm ideas about a child's proper place, and even if she had not, Lady Catherine knew her mother would never permit her to remain. For even though they were all related in some way or other, Wynne was a very grand place, and on the journey here, she had already had to listen to many a lecture on her behavior in such exalted company.

It was all so unfair! As she entered the room she and her sister were to share, she tried to still all these strange feelings of depression and resentment. She did not know what was the matter with her. She had never minded the arrangements before—indeed, she had always thought she had much more fun than Millie did, separated as she was from adult disapproval.

Last year, when she was sixteen, Millie had joined the ranks of grownups, and she had told Lady Catherine all about the long, formal dinners, the necessity of sitting bolt-upright and minding your manners, and of having to converse with elderly relatives who seemed to watch you like a hawk, as if anxious to catch you out in some grievous *faux pas.*

Now Lady Catherine sank down on the window seat and stared out at the cold, dormant gardens of Wynne. It did not matter that they were barely visible in the early winter dusk, for she was not looking at them. Behind her, she could hear Millie giving her maid some breathless instructions, her voice full of anticipation and excitement. It would be four more long years before she herself could join the grownups—four whole years! How was she ever to wait?

In her mind's eye she saw the viscount's handsome face and twinkling eyes. She almost seemed to see him winking at her and nodding, as if he understood, and once again she felt a yearning deep inside. She clenched her hands into fists as she came to a sudden, lightning-quick decision. I am going to marry him, she told herself silently. Someday—somehow—I am going to marry him.

She was not sorry when Millie left for a conference with her mother on the best way to dress her hair that evening, and Betty, the maid, took the blue gown away to press. Now that the large room was quiet, she was able to think.

She knew Lionel Eden was twenty years old, and she

told herself that that was, after all, only eight years older than she was herself. And lots of husbands were older than their wives; why, her own papa was ten years older than her mama! But as she considered it more carefully, she knew those eight years might just as well be a hundred. It had been plain to see that he thought her a child still, the little Miss Kittycat he had called her for years. And until she was older, he would not think of her any other way.

Well, she would just have to grow up as fast as she could, she decided, compressing her lips in determination. And then, someday, he would look at her as he had looked at Millie.

Lady Catherine got up and went to the pier glass to observe herself more carefully than she ever had before. What she saw caused her to sigh deeply in despair. She was reed-thin and very short, most unlike her sister's sweetly curved height. And her heart-shaped face with its pale brows and lashes seemed bland to her, as smooth and expressionless as an egg. She tried a smile, but since she had seldom felt less like smiling, it was a poor effort, and one she felt made her look idiotic. The scowl that replaced it made her ugly. Millie had a pretty smile, and pink lips, and rounded, blushing cheeks. The only unusual feature Lady Catherine could boast was her green eyes, and even those she regarded with loathing. With their slight tilt and yellow flecks, they did look just like a cat's. How awful! And her hair—ugh! Instead of Millie's shining, orderly ringlets, hers was so thick and unruly it defied any arrangement but tight braids. And it was red—*red!* Oh, why hadn't the gods been kinder and divided the looks in the family more evenly? she wondered. Even Emery had smooth blond hair and clear blue eyes, which, as a man, he did not have the slightest use for. It was not at all fair!

As she wandered over to a chair near the fireplace, she frowned again. Because even if she turned out to be a beauty, which she did not in the least expect would happen, it might well be to no avail. It would be seven long years before she made her comeout, and in those years, the viscount might very well fall in love and marry someone else. No, no! she cried out, her hands clasped tightly at her nonexistent bosom. I could not bear it, he must not!

I shall just have to make him wait for me, somehow, she told herself, desperately searching her mind for some way this miracle might be accomplished. And I shall have to keep him away from beautiful ladies until then.

And how are you to do that? the practical side of her nature argued. You only see him here at Wynne, and not even every year at that. And there are so many lovely, grown-up girls. He has probably met dozens of them, and will meet hundreds—no, thousands!—more in seven long years. And, of course, they will all want to marry him, too, he is so handsome, so—so wonderful!

Lady Catherine plopped herself down in the chair, her legs sprawled wide before her and her toes pointed toward the ceiling. It was a position her mother had outlawed, and one she was careful to assume only when she was alone.

Perhaps the best thing to do would be to make him promise to wait for me, she thought. But to obtain that promise, somehow she would have to make him see that she would be worth the wait. And even though she was the daughter of a wealthy marquess, she did not see how she was to accomplish that, considering her nonexistent looks. But perhaps if she saw a lot of him this Christmas, showed him how much she adored him, how charming she was. . . .

Lady Catherine rolled her eyes heavenward. By no stretch of the imagination could she be considered charming, and she knew it only too well. Her brother called her a proper pest and sometimes worse when they were alone, and her mother had despaired of more than her manners, although her father had laughed at her complaints and called her his second son. And as for Millie, even as kind and gentle as she was, she had been upset enough in the past to proclaim her little sister an utter disgrace to the family.

I will just have to prove them all wrong, Lady Catherine told herself. She would learn to be as demure as anyone could wish for, mending her tomboyish ways. And she would seek the viscount's company as often as she could manage it. It was true she could not see him in the evenings, banished as she was to the children's dining salon, but there were all those daytime hours. Perhaps they could ride together. She knew she was an excellent rider, one her father said was good enough to follow the hunt even now. Her expression brightened when she remembered that Millie did not care for riding. And there might be skating, or sleighing parties. And if the weather was inclement, she could ask the viscount to teach her to play billiards, or challenge him to a game of chess. She would not despair.

She heard the first dressing bell ringing, and she rose and stretched, knowing her privacy was almost at an end.

As she unbuttoned her old merino gown, she reminded herself that she must take great pains that no one suspected what she was about, for that would be fatal. Emery and Millie would laugh at her, and her mother and father would be horrified. As for the rest of the family, she knew she would die if they found out. She was sure that awful Garth Allendon would make fun of her unmercifully, and the others her own age would never let her forget it, either. No, what had happened to her since her arrival at Wynne was too important, too precious a secret, to share with anyone. Except—at the right time and place—with Lionel Eden, Viscount Benning.

Several corridors away, dressing for dinner in his

room in the bachelor's wing, that same gentleman asked his valet to adjust the drapes behind him, for he had just felt a distinct and decidedly chilly draft on the back of his neck.

Two

LADY CATHERINE FORCED herself to stay awake that night until Millie came to bed, for she had to find out what had happened between her and the viscount. She had only had a few quick glimpses of him herself when she was summoned to the drawing room after dinner with the other children, and she had been disappointed when she saw him deep in conversation with her sister, not even noticing she had come in. She tried to will him to look her way, but he would not. Her curtsy to the dowager duchess was a little abstracted, therefore, behavior that did not seem to overset the matriarch of the family at all. The dowager was seated in the place of honor before the fire, her son, the current duke, and his duchess in attendance nearby. All the children were paraded forward to make their bows and curtsies before they were swept into her arms for a hearty kiss.

"I remember you, my girl," the dowager said now, leaning forward to peer at Lady Catherine. "How could I ever forget those eyes! You are Kitty Cahill, am I right?"

Remembering her promise to herself to mend her ways, Kitty smiled and nodded. "I hope I find you well, ma'am?" she asked politely in a loud voice. She noticed her mother frowning and putting one finger to her lips, and she sighed. The one, quick darting glance she had dared, had shown that the viscount had not bothered to

23

turn and smile at her, or acknowledge her in any way. And he was so outstanding this evening, too! His dark formal dress fit him to perfection, and above the white of his cravat and high shirt points, his handsome head topped with those thick auburn locks was enough to take your breath away. At least, it was fair to say, it did Lady Catherine Cahill's.

When the dowager excused her, Kitty tried to move in the viscount's direction, but her father took her arm and led her firmly to her mother's side. And there she had been forced to remain until the duchess gave the signal for the children to retire, attended by the Allendon governess. This good lady took them all to a salon some distance away, where they played at spillikins and other silly games until it was time for bed. How disappointed she had been!

In fact, thought Lady Catherine as she yawned hugely, wishing Millie would hurry up, the only pleasant thing that had happened all evening had been when she discovered that Garth Allendon had had his sixteenth birthday and left childish things behind him forever. Or perhaps he had not, she realized, remembering his grin as she passed him in the drawing room, and the little meowing sound he made before he whispered, "Here, Tibby, Tibby!" That was the dreadful nickname he called her, as if she were indeed a cat. Kitty had raised her chin and ignored him. She was beyond Garth Allendon's taunts forever now, and all his immature behavior. She was in love!

When Millie came in at last, Kitty sat up in bed to question her about her evening. Her sister seemed surprised to find her awake, but Kitty did not think she suspected anything. As Betty undressed her and brushed her hair, Millie told all about dinner, her table companions, and the plans that had been made among some of the young guests for a drive to Chalfont St. Giles to see John Milton's cottage. Lady Catherine frowned, already trying to find a way she could be included in the excursion.

"I saw you talking to Viscount Benning when I came into the drawing room, Millie," she remarked next. "Do you like him?"

Her sister was standing now so Betty could lower her nightgown over her head, and Lady Catherine could not gauge her reaction to this question. Through the folds of demure white cotton, Millie said, "I think he is very handsome. And there is something in his eyes. . . ."

Her voice died away before she thanked her maid and dismissed her for the night. As she came and climbed into bed beside her sister, Lady Catherine made herself say, "But Harry Benson is handsome, too, don't you think? And I could see how taken he was with you this afternoon, Millie. And he is older than the viscount, and as rich as rich can be! And he will be an earl someday, you must not forget that!"

Lady Millicent peered at her. "Whatever are you babbling about, Kitty?" she asked in some astonishment.

Lady Catherine made herself shrug before she settled back on her pillows. "Oh, nothing," she said airily. "I just wondered if you have been considering the future, Millie."

Her sister laughed and blew out the candle. As she snuggled under the covers, she murmured, "What a funny little child you are, Kitty! I am not interested in attaching any gentleman, not for a long time. Why, if I did, I would miss my Season in London when I am turned eighteen, and believe me, I have no intention of giving up all that fun and frolic!"

Lady Catherine stared up into the dark, feeling elated for the first time in several hours. Beside her, Lady Millicent murmured her good-nights as she turned over on her side.

In only a few moments, her deeper breathing showed

she was fast asleep. Still Lady Catherine lay quietly, picturing the viscount's handsome face, his beautiful blue eyes. She must make sure that Millie held to her plan for a London Season, she thought, and she must also make sure the viscount did not have any opportunity to get her to change her mind. Kitty did not doubt he could, not for a moment. After all, what were a few months of balls and parties, compared to him? She knew if it were she, she wouldn't give a snap of her fingers for it, if he were to beckon to her. So I must keep him from even thinking of beckoning, no matter what I have to do, she told herself. And I will. Somehow I will.

For a moment, her hands formed into determined fists, and then sleepiness overcame her, and she yawned and closed her eyes. Tomorrow, she told herself. I shall begin tomorrow.

The very next morning, Lady Catherine lingered in the hall for as long as she dared, waiting for the viscount to come down to breakfast. But at last, in spite of her great and intense interest in the former Dukes and Duchesses of Wynne whose portraits adorned the walls there, she was forced to retreat. She was sure not only Summers, the butler, but the footmen as well, were regarding her with deep suspicion.

When she reached the large morning room all the visiting ladies used during their sojourn at Wynne, she discovered her mother was very upset at her absence.

"Didn't Betty tell you I wished to see you right after your breakfast, Kitty? Where have you been?" she asked, as she measured another length of thread for her needlepoint.

"I'm sorry, Mama," Kitty said, hanging her head. She wished she might put the blame on Betty, but she could not bring herself to do that; besides, the maid would be sure to tell her mother she had lied to her. "She did tell me, but I—I forgot. I was investigating Wynne again."

Lady Deane shook her head and pointed to a low stool nearby. "Sit down at once, Kitty, and take up your sampler. Mrs. Holden has promised to read to us as we work."

Kitty did as she was bade. Faintly, through the windows that fronted the east garden, she could hear the laughing conversation of several young men, and she knew she might just as well be here. The viscount had gone out. She might have known he was not the type to linger abovestairs fussing over his attire when he could be riding.

Mrs. Holden's novel was not particularly interesting, chosen as it had been to be suitable for any age, and it was full of dull moral precepts as well. Lady Catherine bent over her sampler with industry her mother could only applaud. Later, when they all rose, she asked her mother if she might not begin some needlepoint, too, or perhaps some embroidery. She had noticed how attractive Millie had looked, sitting at the frame set in a window embrasure nearby. Besides, samplers were only for babies, she thought, although she did not tell her mother that.

"I am pleased you want to, Kitty," Lady Deane said, smiling warmly. "But first you must show a great improvement in your white work, and finish your sampler. You are not expert enough to try anything more difficult as yet."

She turned then, and beckoned to her older daughter. As Millie approached, Kitty admired her pretty primrose morning gown and her neat blond curls. How gracefully she moves, and she has such a shape, too, she thought in some despair. As she sighed a little, Lady Deane said, "It is a lovely day, and not too cold, my dears. I suggest you take advantage of it while you can, and go out for a walk."

Lady Millicent nodded, and Kitty was quick to agree. She knew if she managed to keep Millie outdoors, she might have a chance to intercept the viscount when he returned from his ride. However, the day was brisk enough to make her older sister insist on returning to the palace after only a half hour's exercise, strolling the dormant garden's paths. Miss Regina Holden, who was one of Millie's bosom companions, and who had joined them on their walk, was quick to agree.

"I quite long to show you my new gown, Millie," she said as they made their way back to the impressive front doors of Wynne. "I am sure it is as fine as any London gown, but you shall be the judge. And it is such a pretty color, the palest pink! My Mama says it is stunning with my dark hair."

The two older girls were soon deep in a discussion of gowns and other fripperies, as Lady Catherine trailed disconsolately behind them. The drive remained stubbornly empty; there was no sign of a handsome, godlike horseman cantering toward them.

As they all reached the steps, she had a sudden inspiration. "I think I shall just go around to the kennels before I come in, Millie," she said, her green eyes wide with innocence.

Her sister, intent on a description of her own new ball gown, only waved her hand. As Kitty hurried away before Millie could remember she was responsible for her little sister and insist she come inside, Miss Holden whispered, "Thank heavens! It is so difficult for us to talk, my dear, when that child is with us. And I have the most delicious news which I could not tell you before. Little pitchers and big ears, you know. . . ."

Kitty did not draw a deep breath until she was out of sight around the east wing. She was determined to remain outdoors, no matter how long it took Lionel Eden to return. Besides, she had always enjoyed the kennels, and the jovial kennel master, Mr. Grist.

There was a new litter of puppies for her to admire, and she spent a happy hour playing with them. They were such adorable, uncoordinated woolly balls that she almost forgot her main purpose in coming here. It was only when she heard her brother's voice outside the kennel that she was recalled to the viscount, and hurriedly took her leave of Mr. Grist and his charges.

"Em'ry, wait for me!" she called, running after him. He was accompanied by a trio of young gentlemen, and she could see they had just returned from riding. She decided to ignore the fact that Garth Allendon was one of them.

"What's up, brat?" Emery Cahill asked carelessly as she reached his side, panting a little now.

Lady Catherine could now see the viscount was not among the company, and her heart sank. "Oh, nothing," she said carelessly, in answer to her brother's question. "I just wondered where you had been. Did you have a good ride?"

Her brother stared at her in some amazement, and Garth Allendon snickered. Feeling something more was called for, Kitty made herself add, "I wish you had told me you were going riding! I would have liked to have joined you."

Garth Allendon laughed out loud. "We didn't want you to join us," he said scornfully. "I doubt you could even have kept up with us, on your pony."

Kitty's green eyes glowed golden in her anger. "I do not ride a pony anymore!" she said, her hands on her hips.

Emery Cahill took her arm. "No need to fly up into the boughs, Kitty," he said. "After all, you rode a pony last year. Now, come along. I don't understand what you were doing out here by yourself in the first place. Where's Millie?"

Lady Catherine shrugged and resigned herself to a further wait before a reunion with the viscount. "She's with Regina Holden, talking about clothes, and heaven knows what else," she said crossly.

Lord Harry Benson smiled. "I think we can imagine what else, can't we?" he asked. All the young men laughed.

They had reached a side door now, and Emery Cahill opened it and pushed his little sister inside. " Be off with you, Kitty," he ordered. "Go and find Mama, or Millie."

"Yes, do that," Garth Allendon chimed in. "We certainly don't want you hanging about, bothering us."

Kitty opened her mouth to give him a stunning set-down, but then she remembered her new resolution to become a perfect lady, and she shut it again. As the four young gentlemen stood amazed, she curtsied to them before she turned on her heel and marched away. Behind her, she could hear them murmuring, and that horrid Garth Allendon's snickers, and she concentrated on keeping her head high as she climbed the stairs.

She did not have a chance to search for the viscount again that day, for her mother took her in charge. They both went to the nursery to meet the newest additions to the family, and Lady Deane insisted she play with some of the older children there, and keep them amused. Kitty sat them down and told them a rousing story, something she enjoyed doing as much as they appeared to enjoy hearing it.

And when they quit the nursery at last, she discovered her closest friend, Katherine Elizabeth Rice, had just arrived with her mother for the holidays, and she went with her to her room to help her unpack while they exchanged news.

The young lady was always called by both her names, for Catherine, no matter how it was spelled, was a popular choice of name throughout the family. Thus, although there was a profusion of nicknames—Kitty, and Cat, and Kath—Mrs. Rice, being an extremely proper and formal person, would not allow her daughter to be called by a diminutive.

Miss Rice was a year Kitty's junior, and in the years they had both been coming to Wynne, the two girls had become good friends. Since they were close in age, they were thrown into each other's company a great deal, and both being incorrigible tomboys, had discovered they liked the same activities.

Now Kitty sat on the window seat and watched Katherine Elizabeth as she helped one of the maids unpack her trunk.

"I suppose that my awful cousin Garth is here, isn't he?" she asked, her blue gray eyes sparkling.

Kitty nodded, envying her friend's ash-blond hair. "Yes, he is, but he is sixteen now, and so he has joined the grownups," she said.

Miss Rice sighed. "Well, that's something, anyway. Do you remember how he teased us last year, Kitty?"

Lady Catherine nodded. "He is still doing it," she said, her voice gloomy. "And last night, when I went into the drawing room after dinner, he called me Tibby!"

Miss Rice tossed her braids. "I hate him," she said with fervor, oblivious to the maid who had served the Allendons for years. "But I have a wonderful plan, Kitty," she said as she dropped a pile of hair ribbons on the bed and came over to the window seat to whisper to her friend. As she sat down, she picked up Kitty's hands and squeezed them. "How would it be if we played a trick on him to pay him back, a really good trick?" she asked, her breathless whisper full of deviltry.

"What kind of trick?" Kitty asked, her green eyes lighting up as she forgot her intention to put such childish things behind her forever.

Miss Rice leaned closer and whispered in her ear, and as the maid watched them both indulgently, she saw that even with both hands over her mouth, that Lady Kitty could not contain her giggles.

"Katherine Elizabeth! We can't! What if our mothers find out, or—or anybody else?" Kitty asked, suddenly remembering the viscount's handsome face and form. If he were to learn she was involved in this plot to mortify the duke's youngest son, he might laugh, but the deed would only reinforce his opinion that she was just a child. Proper, grownup young ladies never invaded the bachelor wing, certainly not to short-sheet the youngest Allendon's bed and put a white mouse in it as well.

"But I brought the mouse all the way from London," Katherine Elizabeth was insisting now, a little bewildered. "And it was such a chore keeping it a secret from my mama! If she had not been so preoccupied with Pug, who is ailing, she must have noticed all the rustling in my bandbox and demanded to know what was going on. It is too bad! Why can't we do it?"

"Only children behave so," Kitty said, somewhat lamely. "We are too old for such childish pranks now."

Miss Rice's little pink mouth fell open in astonishment. This was Kitty Cahill, the most daredevil girl she had ever known? And it was such a marvelous plan, too! She had been looking forward to hiding nearby with Kitty, to listen to Lord Allendon's shrieks when his bare feet encountered the mouse in his suddenly shortened bed.

"I never thought *you* would be so stuffy, Kitty," she said now, her eyes accusing. "And whatever am I to do with the mouse?"

Kitty shrugged. "I don't know," she said. "You can't give it to one of the little boys, or we might well find it in one of our own beds some night. I know! Why don't you just let it loose in the conservatory? It's warm there, and it will probably find other mice and be happy."

Miss Rice rose, her head averted. She had looked forward so to seeing her friend again, and playing this marvelous trick on their sworn enemy together. But now it appeared that Kitty had become as prim as the grownups. As she went to put her hair ribbons away, Katherine Elizabeth wondered why that was so, for Kitty was only twelve to her eleven, and would not be a grownup for years and years yet.

Her mother's bustling entrance interrupted her thoughts, and she was forced to excuse herself so she could change her traveling dress for tea. As she did so, she wondered if she had imagined Kitty's hasty retreat, almost as if she had been glad to leave her, and she shook her head.

As she hurried down the stairs, Kitty felt a pang of guilt. Katherine Elizabeth was her best friend, and she was sorry she had had to squash her wonderful plan, because now her life had changed. She realized suddenly that trying to be a grownup was not any fun at all, but all these depressing thoughts left her mind as she saw the viscount and her sister Millie entering the front hall below her.

She had spied them walking toward the palace from Katherine Elizabeth's window, and she had been quick to make her escape as soon as Mrs. Rice had come in. Kitty had not known the viscount was with Millie, but it obviously behooved her to join them both as quickly as possible. As she reached the bottom of the flight, she saw them moving in the direction of the library, and she called out to them.

As she hurried toward them, she wondered if she had imagined the little look of impatience that seemed to cross both their faces before it was quickly hidden.

"There you are, Millie! I have been looking all over for you," she said as she skidded to a halt beside them. "I give you good afternoon, m'lord," she added, dropping into her best curtsy.

"Is Mama looking for me?" Millie asked, a little frown between her brows.

"Oh, no," Kitty said as she managed to insert herself between them. "It was just that I wondered what you were doing."

Lady Millicent stared down at her red braids, and then she looked helplessly at the viscount. She saw him shake his head a little and wink, and she blushed. They had spent an enjoyable hour walking about the park, and she was not at all pleased to have her little sister interrupting their *tête à tête*. Lionel Eden was a very

handsome young man, and she could tell he was in a fair
way to being smitten with her.

"I am especially glad to see you, m'lord," Kitty was
saying now. "I have been longing to ask you all about
your adventures in the Indies. It must have been so
exciting! Do say you will tell me all about it, if you
please?"

The viscount was not proof against her pleading green
eyes, and he grinned down at her. "Very well, Miss
Kittycat. Oh, no, it is Lady Catherine now, is it not? I
forgot, and I beg you to forgive me for being so
gauche."

Kitty had no idea what being gauche was, but she was
quick to assure the viscount that she forgave him,
shutting her mouth firmly to prevent herself from
adding she would be happy to forgive him anything in
the world, anything at all.

She stayed with them until the first dressing bell
sounded, in spite of Millie's less than subtle hints that
she take herself off, and even when others came into the
library, she did not relax her vigil. The viscount had told
them both a great deal about Jamaica, but Kitty had not
liked the little smiles he and her sister had exchanged on
occasion, or some of the remarks that he made that she
could not understand yet Millie seemed to find so
amusing. She told herself she must pay more attention
to her lessons and set herself a program of reading, so
that the next time they met, he would not be able to talk
over her head.

As she climbed the stairs beside her sister, a small but
doggedly persistent watchdog, Kitty decided that as
soon as she returned home, she would ask her governess
to procure some books about the West Indies. Surely
knowing more about the place Lionel Eden had spent so
much time in, could only impress him.

When she came into the drawing room later that
evening, Katherine Elizabeth beside her, she overheard
her father and brother discussing taking an early-

morning ride with some of the other gentlemen, and she made up her mind to join them. She had no idea if the viscount would be there, but she was having such little luck intercepting him here in the palace, it was obvious she must try other methods. And she had not liked the looks he and Millie had exchanged, nor the way her sister seemed so annoyed with her for remaining with them. Could it be possible that Millie was abandoning her plans for a London Season? All the time Betty was helping her to dress, Kitty sat on the bed and enthused about London, and how wonderful it would be when Millie was there at last. But Millie had only looked impatient, and her blue eyes were still stormy even when they all went down to dinner.

Kitty was delighted to see that Lionel Eden intended to be one of the riding party the next morning. She sat up straighter on her chestnut mare when he appeared, and sent him an adoring smile as she waved her crop in greeting. And silently she gave a prayer of thanksgiving that her father had only laughed at her mother when she had insisted it was not proper for Kitty to ride with the men.

"Come now, Rose," he had chided her as Kitty hid her crossed fingers in the pocket of her robe. They were all in Lady Deane's sitting room where Kitty had waited patiently until her parents came up to bed. "What's the harm then?" Lord Deane had added. "Kitty is a child still, even if she is an accomplished horsewoman. It will be good for her to get some exercise, and I shall be proud to show off her riding. I think I can promise she won't hold us up, can't I, Kitty?"

Kitty was fervent in her assurances that she would be on her best behavior, and Lady Deane had capitulated at last.

Now Kitty wished her habit was newer, and that she could have one trimmed with fur, like Millie's was. But she forgot such sartorial problems as the riding party set off down the drive. She would have liked to take a position beside the viscount, but only a little consideration persuaded her that this would be most unwise. She must not call attention to herself, or her attachment for him, not with her father and brother so near. Accordingly, she rode demurely beside Lord Deane, and it was only later, as they returned home, that she found an opportunity to speak to Lionel Eden.

"How well you ride, Lady Catherine," he said, reining in beside her as everyone slowed for the turn into the main gates.

Kitty smiled her thanks for the compliment, suddenly breathless and tongue-tied again.

The viscount thought her a taking child, especially on horseback, with her pale heart-shaped face flushed from the cold air and her big green eyes sparkling. "Do you hunt as well?" he asked.

A shadow crossed her face. "Not yet," she admitted. "There is some stupid rule . . ." She paused then, and bit her lower lip. "I shall follow the hunt soon, however," she went on quickly. "My father has promised I may."

"You will enjoy riding cross country, I know, for it is plain to see that you are the type of rider who throws her heart first over every obstacle," the viscount assured her.

Kitty longed to tell him that she had already thrown her heart—in his direction—but she forced herself to keep silent.

She tried to stay with the party after they had all dismounted so she might discover what the viscount meant to do for the remainder of the day, but her father dismissed her firmly. Riding was one thing, but consorting with a group of men intent on a bumper of ale and perhaps some warm conversation, was another.

Kitty spent the rest of the day dodging her mother, and trying to attach herself first to Millie, and then to Emery. To say that both of them were less than pleased at this sudden longing for their company, would be an understatement.

When she would have settled down with Millie and her friend Regina Holden in one of the smaller salons where they were sitting and chatting, she was ordered away at once. "You have become closer than my own shadow," Millie told her, her gentle voice petulant. "Besides, Katherine Elizabeth is looking for you. Go!"

And in the billiard room where she found her brother Emery showing Garth Allendon a special trick shot, she was told to make herself scarce as well. "Be off with you at once, Kitty," Emery Cahill said in a low undertone. "This is no place for you! Go and play with the other children!"

Kitty was forced to abandon her efforts, for that day at least. She was also forced to listen to a cataloging of her shortcomings that same evening when the entire family gathered before dinner in Lady Deane's sitting room. It had been their custom to do so, so they might exchange any private family news.

"You'll have to do something about Kitty, Mama!" Emery exclaimed as he paced the room. "She is a perfect pest, always dogging my footsteps and appearing where she should not be. I cannot for the life of me figure out what's come over her!"

"Nor I," Millie said before her mother could speak. "Why, I have to order her away if I want a moment alone with my friends. She is constantly underfoot, and it is too bad!"

Lady Deane was not at all averse to Kitty's dogging Millie's footsteps, for she felt her to be a wonderful, albeit unwitting, chaperone, but she could not like her youngest daughter bothering the gentlemen. Until the dinner gong sounded, therefore, she proceeded to read Kitty a lecture, and set down rules about where she could go, and with whom, and to order her to cease badgering her elders. Kitty agreed at last, but in her

breast there burned a great resentment. However was
she to attach the wonderful viscount if she could not get
anywhere near him? she wondered.

When she was finally in bed later, she made herself a
promise. Since she was to be denied his company, except
by the veriest accident, she would just have to rely on
prayer. She would pray, and fervently, too, both night
and morning, that Lionel Eden would escape her sister's
wiles. And somehow, by some divine intervention that
she would earnestly entreat, he would be saved as well
from all other women, until she herself came of age.

Three

IN SOME STRANGE way, Kitty was almost relieved to return to the childhood she had abandoned during the following days. It was all so much more comfortable, playing with Katherine Elizabeth, visiting the nursery to tell stories to the little children and romp with them, and most importantly, be able to relax and forget the grownup manners she had been trying so hard to emulate. And she was glad to see how much happier Katherine Elizabeth was, now her friend spent more time with her.

She saw the viscount occasionally, and she was glad that he frequently had a warm smile for her, or a pleasant word.

But no matter how much better she felt, behaving like the child she still was, she never forgot her love for him, and she prayed as hard as she had promised herself she would, to keep him safe. She was not able to see him with Millie any more, and when she questioned her sister, she learned very little about any attraction Millie might be feeling for Lionel Eden. Lady Millicent had become strangely reticent on the subject.

Kitty did not try to gain her mother's permission to go on the drive to Chalfont St. Giles that had been planned. No children had been invited, nor any elders either, although Millie told her with a toss of her head that the duchess insisted on sending two spinster cousins with them, as chaperones.

But the morning of the excursion, the guests at Wynne woke to discover a major snowstorm had begun sometime during the night—a storm that did not cease until afternoon. Millie was disappointed. Of course there could be no thought of going now when the roads were impassable, and Kitty sent up a fervent thank-you in her morning prayers and went down to breakfast with an especially good appetite.

By early afternoon, when the snow stopped falling, she and Katherine Elizabeth had made their plans. There were a number of sleds in the stables, and they were looking foward to sliding down the steep hill below the north face of Wynne. Several younger children had begged to join them as well, and Kitty promised the Allendon governess that she would keep an eye on them.

Everyone had a wonderful time. It was not too cold, and the air was still, so there was no danger of anyone's taking a chill. Time and time again, she and Katherine Elizabeth pulled their sled up the snowy slope, and helped the little ones before they rode down together, the speed of their passage whipping their excited shrieks away.

Kitty spared an occasional glance at the palace. She knew Millie was spending the afternoon with her mother and the other ladies, and she did not envy her one little bit. She wondered if Millie ever looked out the window and wished she might join in the fun.

Suddenly her heart leapt, and she felt a warm glow as she saw the viscount coming toward them, followed by some of the other young men. They were dragging a large sled that Kitty had never seen before.

"M'lord," she called, smiling at him from where she stood at the top of the slope, and wishing that she did not feel she needed to wipe her nose. "I am surprised to see you here—er, all of you."

Beside her, Katherine Elizabeth poked her, hard, and

she looked around, surprising a sheepish look on Garth Allendon's face. He seemed very embarrassed to be caught here with the children. Her friend giggled behind her mittens.

"I could not resist, Lady Catherine," the viscount told her. "After all, I have not seen snow for two long years, and I remember only too well how wonderful sledding is. You don't object to us joining you, do you?"

Kitty shook her head as Garth Allendon said, his voice haughty, "Much good it would do her if she did! This is *my* family's property. She is only a guest here."

"Do try for a little more conduct, Garth," the viscount admonished him as he knelt to position the sled. "Now, who goes with me first?" he asked. "Since it was my idea we come out, I have appropriated a seat on the first run."

The sled was quickly filled with three others, and they pushed off. Kitty watched them, lost in reverie, until Katherine Elizabeth asked her if she intended to stand there until she froze. At that, she took her seat on their own sled, and followed her heart down the steep slope.

Some of the young men only stayed for a little while, but Lionel Eden remained until the children's nurses came out to fetch them. He had taken first one, and then another before him on the big sled, for it went much faster than theirs. Kitty envied each and every one of them as they leaned against his broad chest, and were protected in the circle of his strong arms.

As the children were being led away, protesting the end of the fun and assuring their nurses they were not a bit cold, and couldn't they please just have one more run, Kitty took a deep breath. She could tell by the way the viscount was brushing off his clothes and looking toward the palace that he intended to go in soon as well, and the thought that she was soon to lose his company made her bold.

"Won't you please take me down on the big sled, too, m'lord?" she begged. "It looks such fun!"

The viscount laughed. "Very well, Miss Kittycat, but only if you promise to help me drag it up again," he said.

Kitty nodded, her throat so tight with joy she could not speak. As Katherine Elizabeth stared at her in astonishment, she went and sat down on the sled. A moment later, she felt Lionel Eden settle down behind her, and then his arms came around her to take hold of the steering rope, and his legs imprisoned her, one on either side of her body. She could feel his warm breath on her cheek, and she felt a little dizzy.

"Hold tight, now!" he ordered as he pushed off.

Kitty closed her eyes as she leaned back so she was resting against him. As the sled gathered speed down the hill, she told herself she had never been so happy in her entire life, no, not even when Papa had given her the chestnut mare, or when Mama had relented and told her she did not have to eat brussels sprouts anymore.

At the bottom of the slope, when the sled finally coasted to a halt, she remained where she was. The viscount hugged her a little before he got to his feet. "Ride's over, m'lady," he said. When she did not reply, he added, "Has the cat got your tongue?"

Kitty made herself get up as well. "No, it just took my breath away," she said, going to take hold of the rope with him and helping him turn the sled around. "How much faster it goes than the little sleds! It was wonderful!"

Kitty hoped with all her heart that Lionel Eden would suggest another run, but he only grinned at her. "Perhaps we can do it again tomorrow?" she asked as they trudged up the slope. She wished it were twice as long.

"I might be forgiven my lapse today, Lady Catherine, but I must look to my dignity tomorrow," he told her.

She admired the white puffs that came from his mouth as he spoke, and his ruddy, handsome face, those brilliant blue eyes. If only I were taller, she thought, I would be that much closer to him!

"But what a shame," she made herself say lightly. "Can't grownups have any fun?"

When she saw the little smile that curled his lips, and he did not answer, she added, "But you are not so very grownup, you know. You are only eight years older than I am, and that is not a great difference at all. Don't you agree? Why, my Papa is ten years older than my Mama!"

What the viscount might have replied to this ingenuous remark, she never found out, for they had reached the top of the slope then. Kitty saw that Katherine Elizabeth was looking at her almost accusingly, and she realized she should have asked her to join them. But she knew she was not a bit sorry she had not. How wonderful it had been to be alone with him, and close, even for these few minutes.

"I think we should go in now, ladies, for it is almost time for tea," the viscount said. "Hop on the sled, and I'll give you a ride to the front steps. You can trail your sled behind."

Kitty wanted to help him pull it, but when she saw Katherine Elizabeth's face brighten, she took her seat behind her without a word.

Although Kitty spent a lot of time watching the approach to the sledding hill the next day, Viscount Benning did not come and join the children, nor did he do so in the days that followed. And even when Kitty suggested they all build an enormous snowman right in front of the billiard room windows, he did not appear to help. And it isn't as if it is beneath his dignity, either, she thought darkly. Why, the duke himself had helped them lift the heavy ball that was the snowman's head in place, and sent one of the boys scurrying to get two coals for eyes, a carrot for a nose, and a sprig of holly for the mishapen old hat he had brought out to crown their creation. And if the duke, who was as old as her father, didn't consider making a snowman silly and childish, who was Lionel Eden to think otherwise?

That evening, when she went into the drawing room for the nightly audience with the dowager duchess, that elderly lady peered at her and smiled. "I have been watching you, Kitty Cahill," she said. "You are a good girl to play with the little children, very good indeed. Isn't she, Marjorie?"

The duchess smiled and agreed. When she turned away to speak to the butler, the dowager beckoned Kitty closer "Perhaps you are as good with dogs as children, missy?" she asked, pushing one of her daughter-in-law's favorite sheep dogs away from her feet. "I would so appreciate it if you could get this animal to leave me alone!"

Surprised, Kitty looked down to see the dog licking the dowager's black satin slippers and wagging his tail frantically as he did so. As she bent to grab his collar, she said, "But maybe if you would just pat him, he *would* let you alone, ma'am."

The dowager stared at her, and she added a little shyly, "He is only trying to make you like him. And if you show you do, he will not be so attentive."

Her grace reached out a thin, elegant hand to gingerly pat the huge dog on his shaggy head. "Do you know, Kitty, I have never once seen their eyes," she confided. "To me, they look ridiculous, like overgrown mops!"

As the dog woofed in joy, she added, "Yes, yes, no doubt I have insulted you and your illustrious bloodlines, sir, but one thing I do know. You don't speak English!"

Kitty giggled, and as the duchess turned back to see what the commotion was, she and the dowager exchanged smiles of conspiracy.

Suddenly, she heard Lionel Eden's hearty laugh from across the drawing room and she turned to stare at him. He was in a group that included her sister Millie and Regina Holden, and they seemed to be having a very good time.

As the duchess beckoned another child foward, the dowager leaned forward and whispered, "Do not be in such a hurry to grow up, Kitty Cahill. You will be old for a long, long time, so enjoy your childhood while you can."

Lady Catherine's green eyes widened as she curtsied. Had the dowager duchess seen her gazing at Viscount Benning? Was it possible that she suspected her love for him? Pray not!

She went to sit beside her mother, her eyes lowered. It seemed to her that for all the dowager's failing eyesight, she saw a great deal more than others, and she wished with all her heart that she did not.

As December twenty-fifth grew nearer, the huge stone palace became a very busy place indeed. The servants brought in armloads of fir and holly to decorate the stairs and mantels. Kitty had always loved the fresh, sharp scent of the greens, and the way the fat red candles looked, set among them.

She overheard Regina Holden giggling with her sister about the old custom of placing a slipper on either side of the bed, and putting rosemary in one and thyme in the other. It was believed that if a single girl slept on her back after doing so at the Christmas Season, she would dream of the man she would marry. Kitty did not dare try it, although she longed to do so, for then Millie would find out her secret and tease her unmercifully. Of course, Millie set out her slippers one night, but she would not tell Kitty anything about her dreams the next morning, no matter how she begged.

As was the family custom, everyone from the dowager herself to the littlest toddler had made a trip to the kitchens when the Christmas plum puddings were made. And each one took a turn stirring the pudding, under the cook's watchful eye. It had to be done in a clockwise direction, for everyone knew that to go widdershins meant bad luck in the new year. And as they stirred, they made a secret wish. Kitty, of course, said the prayer that was becoming so familiar to her.

One snowy afternoon, the kissing ball was made. It consisted of two large hoops, one thrust through the other. Each hoop was garlanded with sprigs of evergreen and holly, and decorated with colored ribbons, paper roses, and apples and oranges. Inside it, the duchess carefully placed three tiny figures, to represent the nativity scene, and just before it was hung in a prominent spot in the drawing room, a large bunch of mistletoe was tied to the bottom. There was a great deal of laughter and many gay threats made as the mistletoe was attached. Kitty saw the viscount bend to whisper to her sister, and the way Millie smiled and blushed, and she felt a little, cold chill. She would have gone over and interrupted them, but she was afraid the dowager would notice.

Late in the afternoon on Christmas Eve, all the younger guests went out to drag the yule log home. A large oak had been cut down earlier, and ropes attached to the stump. As they pulled it back to Wynne, they sang Christmas carols. Kitty had managed to be included in the festivity, and she was quick to position herself behind the viscount, pulling on his rope. She was glad that although he laughed and joked with the others, he spoke to her as well, and although it was very cold that afternoon, she felt warm clear through. When they reached the palace, she lingered after the others for a moment to make a Christmas wish on the evening star. It shone clear and bright, low on the western horizon that was still flushed with the sunset's afterglow.

The yule log was placed in the fireplace in the great hall, and lit by the duke with great ceremony. He used a faggot that had been saved from last year's log, lest the house burn down. Everyone watched anxiously as it caught fire, for tradition had it that if the yule log did not burn or at least smolder for twelve hours, it meant bad luck.

On Christmas morning, the Cahills gathered in their own sitting room to exchange gifts. Kitty received a pretty new dress and matching cloak, as well as some books and a paint set. It was a happy time, and when they dressed in their best and went down to join the others going to church, merry greetings were exchanged.

Christmas dinner was served in the early afternoon, and for once, the entire family assembled in the largest salon. The children oohed and aahed as the boar's head was carried in, garnished with sprigs of rosemary and an apple in its mouth. Kitty was much more interested in the goose and roasted potatoes, the glistening preserves and steaming bowls of gravy. The festive meal ended with plum puddings, topped with holly and aflame with brandy.

Later, everyone played games: musical chairs, forfeits, bob apple, and blindman's buff. And when the younger children were borne protesting back to the nursery, yawning and sticky with sweets, the duke called for a large bowl of punch. Kitty knew she couldn't have any, for the punch, besides containing lemons and oranges, was heavily laced with rum, brandy, and ale. She took a deep breath of the heady fumes, thinking it smelled delicious.

And then a large shallow bowl was brought in, and amid much teasing and laughter, filled with a pile of raisins. All the younger guests gathered around, as it was doused in brandy and set aflame.

"Snap Dragon!" Lord Deane exclaimed. "Why, I

had forgotten that old game. Mind you watch your fingers, Millie," he called.

As the participants snatched a raisin or two, as quickly as they could to avoid getting burned, they chanted the verses that went with the game. "Take care you don't take too much, be not greedy in your clutch, Snip! Snap! Dragon! With his blue and lapping tongue, many of you will be stung, Snip! Snap! Dragon!"

"Oh, I got burned!" Millie cried, pulling her hand away and shaking it. "And I am out of the game!"

She put her fingers in her mouth and licked them, as the others laughed at her. But Kitty saw the way Lionel Eden took that hand and kissed it as if to make it better a short time later, and she saw the light in his blue eyes as he did so. And she also saw him catch Millie under the mistletoe and give her a hearty kiss, right on her lips. Suddenly, all Kitty's joy in Christmas disappeared, and her green eyes glowed golden in her disappointment.

She was not sorry when her mother sent her to bed, just as another bowl of punch was brought in and the gentlemen began riddling.

But although she crossed the room as slowly as she could, and lingered under the kissing ball, the viscount did not notice. Instead, all she got for her pains was a taunting "meow" from Garth Allendon, before he whispered, "Scat, Tibby!"

It was too bad! She was wearing a pretty gold dress and matching hair ribbons, too. She thought she looked almost pretty, but as she went up the stairs, she knew she could never, ever, compare to Millie.

Lady Catherine Cahill cried herself to sleep that Christmas night.

Boxing Day dawned clear and cold. There was a gala ball planned for the evening, with neighbors invited to swell the ranks of the houseguests. Millie was in a state of excitement all day, having her hair washed and curled, and fussing over her new ballgown. Kitty lay on her stomach across the bed and watched her as she dressed. She had to admit Millie looked marvelous in her white silk, with its low neckline and tiny sleeves showing off her round arms and bosom, and her golden curls shining in the candlelight.

After her sister had left at last, in a whirl of skirts, Kitty remembered that she and Katherine Elizabeth had made plans to hide on the balcony overlooking the ballroom. It was the first time they had dared to do this, although they had been talking about it for two years. Kitty knew they would be in total disgrace if they were spotted there, but she didn't care. She had to see Lionel Eden in his formal dress, and watch him dance, no matter what risks she had to take to do so.

As she went along the halls and down a flight of stairs toward the ballroom, she heard the orchestra playing, and she paused to listen. It sounded so festive, so gay! How she would love to be there, by some miracle all grown up and so beautiful the viscount must admire her! She leaned her elbows on the railing, her chin in her hands as she dreamed.

Viscount Benning, coming from his rooms in the bachelor's wing, grinned when he spotted her there. He had spilled some sauce on his sleeve at dinner and had retired to his room so his valet could attend to it. Now he was in a hurry to join the other dancers, yet for some reason, he paused and watched Miss Kittycat's little rear end swaying to the music, and the way she was tapping her foot. She was such a funny little thing, he had to keep himself from laughing out loud at her.

"M'lady," he said, coming closer at last.

Kitty spun around, almost losing her balance in her surprise. Her hands went to her mouth. "Why—why, it's you!" she exclaimed, stunned by her good fortune.

The viscount bowed to her. "May I have the honor of this dance, Lady Catherine?" he asked as formally as if she were the Queen.

As he held out his hand, Kitty moved toward him. He is so beautiful, she thought with an ache in her throat. His dark evening clothes fit him to perfection, and above his white linen, his handsome face was full of smiling tenderness. Lion! It was a perfect name for him, with his thick mane of tawny hair, and easy, masculine grace.

As he took her hand, bending down to slide one arm around her shoulders, Kitty came to her senses.

"But—but I don't know how to dance, m'lord," she managed to get out, so disappointed she wanted to cry.

The viscount's brows rose. "That is a problem," he said. "However, I know just how to solve it."

Before she knew what he was about, he let her go, but only so he could pick her up in his arms. As her own arms crept around his neck, he began to dance, spinning her around and humming to the music. Kitty dared to touch his hair, her hand trembling a little as she did so. She wished the music would go on and on, but all too soon, it ended, and the viscount put her down and bowed.

"Now, wasn't that fun?" he asked with a white grin. Then he bowed again. "Someday, when you are grown up, I shall ask you to dance again, but now you must excuse me."

Kitty curtsied before she watched him run lightly down the stairs, toward the gay throng, the lively music —and her beautiful sister Millicent.

When Katherine Elizabeth came to find her a few moments later, she discovered her friend had lost all interest in the ball, and their plans. Her eyes were puzzled as Kitty excused herself, claiming she had a stomachache and must go right to bed.

In reality, Kitty knew she could not bear to watch Lionel Eden now, with any other lady. She wanted to be alone, so she might dream of how wonderful it had felt to be held in his arms, his warm breath stirring in her hair, and the lotion he used making her a little faint. And his cheek had been so near! She might have kissed it, if only she had dared!

The days seemed to rush by after that, and Kitty wished she might hold them back. In no time at all, they would be going home, and she would see Lionel Eden no more. She knew he was planning to return to his father's estate after his stay at Wynne, and that he had invited her brother Emery to visit him there in the spring, before the Season began.

She was out walking one dismal afternoon, thinking about what a long time it would be before next Christmas, when she saw her sister and the viscount a little distance away. They were standing close together near a large elm. She noticed they were out of sight of the palace, and she wondered what they were doing there. Millie hated the cold; it was most unlike her to be out.

Then, to her horror, she saw the viscount take her sister's chin in his big hand, and lift it. He stared down into her face for a moment, and then he bent his head and kissed her, his arms coming around her to pull her close and caress her. Kitty gasped. This was not the kind of kiss he had given Millie under the kissing ball, and this one seemed to go on and on. As she watched, horrified, Millie melted against him in surrender. Startled now, Kitty picked up her skirts and ran toward them.

"Millie, where are you?" she called after she had dodged behind a hedge, for she did not want them to know she had seen their embrace.

When she reached their sides, they had stepped apart, but she could tell from Millie's expression that her interruption was most unwelcome.

She stayed with them, chatting gaily over the ache in her heart, until they were forced by the cold to return to Wynne. That night she stopped thinking about how quickly the time of their visit was passing. Now she could not wait to leave Wynne, and separate Lionel Eden from her sister.

The Cahills returned to Devon a week later. In the days before their departure, Kitty noticed that her mother kept Millie close to her, and she was glad. She wondered if Mama had seen something, too, or if she suspected anything? For although she had wanted badily to tell her mother about that secret meeting and the fervent kiss that had been exchanged, she had not been able to bring herself to do so. She had never been a tattletale, and, even for the viscount, she found she could not be one now.

Lionel Eden came out with them to the carriage the morning they left, although they had said their good-byes to their host and hostess and the other guests at breakfast. Kitty watched him hug Lady Deane and kiss her on the cheek, before he went to Millie and took her hand in his as he wished her a safe trip home. She saw her sister blush, and she was glad when her father said, "Get in the carriage now, ladies! We must not keep the horses standing about in the cold, and we have a long way to go."

Everyone began to obey. As the viscount moved back to the steps, blowing her a casual kiss, Kitty realized suddenly that she could not leave him—not like this. Spinning around, she ran back to him, while her family watched, somewhat bemused by her behavior.

Lionel Eden bent down to hear what she wanted to say when she tugged his sleeve, and he was surprised when she stood on tiptoe so she could speak to him, and him alone.

"Wait for me!" she whispered fiercely, her voice shaking a little in her urgency. "I'll grow up as fast as I can, and you *must* wait for me! I—I love you!"

And then she was gone, running back to the carriage before her father could think to reprimand her, or her mother call.

More than slightly stunned by her revelation and impassioned command, the viscount remained where he was, almost forgetting to wave as the carriages pulled away.

Four

LADY CATHERINE CAHILL did not so much as set eyes on Viscount Benning again for three long years. Due to a sudden change of plans, the Cahills had not gone to London that spring. Lady Deane had not seen the kiss in the garden that Kitty had, but she had noticed the viscount and Millie embracing on another occasion, and she had seen the way Millie flirted with both my lords Benson as well. She was much displeased. If Millie's head was turned so easily by any handsome beau, perhaps she would benefit from a little more maturity before she braved the ranks of the *ton,* she thought. Lady Deane had every intention of arranging an advantageous marriage for her beautiful daughter, and certainly one that did not involve scandal and gossip.

Kitty was as disappointed as her sister when she learned of the postponement, but both girls knew from their mother's tone of voice, and her severe expression, that this was not something they could plead or tease for.

The following December, Lord Deane contracted a serious case of influenza, and they had been forced to cancel their regular Christmas visit to Wynne. Kitty was beginning to feel a little desperate. Of course she was sorry her dear papa was ill, and she knew he had not done it deliberately, but she could not help but deplore his timing. Even Emery remained in Devon, although she had thought that he at least might go and join the family festivities, and be able to tell her all about the viscount when he returned.

And when her spirits revived as winter waned, and plans were finally made to move the family to London for Millie's debut, Emery had a letter from Lionel Eden announcing his immediate departure for Jamaica. His uncle had been seriously injured in an accident at the mill, and his aunt had begged him to come and help her run the plantation until he was completely recovered. He had no idea how long he would be gone.

Kitty was disconsolate at the news. She felt as if a malevolent spirit was keeping them apart, and laughing at her as it did so. And how on earth was she ever to attach Lion if she never got to see him?

As it turned out, it did not matter that the viscount had gone abroad. The death of one of Lady Deane's sisters and the subsequent mourning period, put paid to any comeout for Lady Millicent that spring. Kitty did not give a snap of her fingers about it now, but her sister wailed that she would be left on the shelf without ever getting a chance to get off it.

As more and more time passed, Kitty found she was having trouble remembering Lionel Eden with any clarity, and she was horrified. Why, one night as she climbed into bed after saying her prayers, which as always, included a fervent plea for his continued bachelorhood, she realized she could not recall the exact color of his eyes. And after only a little more reflection, she had to admit she could not bring to mind how his voice sounded when he spoke, or laughed, either.

And yet she knew she loved him still; that she would always love him. And someday—no matter how far away that day was to be—she would make him love her, too. But it was very, very hard to wait.

Trying to cheer herself up, she told herself that it really was better that the viscount did not see her again until she was older, for no matter how hard she tried to grow up faster, she was still a child.

When she had first returned from Wynne, she had set herself to gaining weight. She was sure that if she were not so thin, she would develop the figure Millie had. But all her excess eating had done was to make her feel sick and become pudgy in all the wrong places, so she had abandoned that plan.

She was growing taller, however. She had asked Millie to measure her against a door jamb in her room, and every month she stood against that mark and held her breath. For a long time she remained the same height, but then, suddenly, she began to shoot up. The first time the pencil mark was an inch higher, she had seized her sister's hand and whirled her around the room, chortling with delight.

"But why is it so important, my dear?" Lady Deane had asked, somewhat bewildered, after the matter had been explained to her when she had come in to see what all the merriment was about.

Kitty could not tell her the real reason, of course, but she did say in a fervent voice, "I am determined not to be a little dab of a girl! I *must* grow taller, I must!"

Her mother had laughed then, and assured her that time would take care of the problem. "In fact, my dear Kitty, I expect you to exceed Millie's height," she said. "Do consider your hands and feet. They are almost as large as your sister's now. But you shall see."

As the months passed, Kitty did see. And when she started her menses, she was further delighted to discover that her figure began to develop all by itself, with no help from her at all. Of course, she in no way compared with Lady Millicent's voluptuous curves, but at least, now she went in and out in the proper places, she did not look a complete child anymore.

All her new dresses were much longer, and she only wore her hair in braids during the day, for convenience. She had even been allowed to join the hunt at last, and in her new, form-fitting habit, she felt very grownup indeed.

From his occasional letters to Emery, she knew the viscount was still unmarried, and continued to reside in Jamaica. And perhaps, she told herself, that was just as well, for surely there could not be many lovely English girls on the island, and he would not be in London when Lady Millicent was presented to the *ton*.

Although she knew, at just-turned fifteen, she would not be permitted to attend any evening parties, Kitty was sure there would be something she could do to help her sister find a suitable gentleman, and get her engaged before the viscount returned. As fiercely as any matchmaking mama, Kitty was determined to promote an advantageous marriage for her sister as soon as they reached town. Then Millie would pose no threat to her own happiness.

Besides, it was not as if Millie was pining away because she had been deprived of the viscount's company and kisses. She never mentioned him anymore, and Kitty could tell by the way she flirted with every handsome gentleman that crossed her path, that Millie had not been in love with him at all. She felt a great deal better when she reached this conclusion, for she had not liked thinking she might have to cause Millie any pain. Not that I would not have done so in a minute, if it had come to that, she admitted to herself as she settled down with the latest romance.

Earlier, she had tried to mend her ways, startling her governess considerably by her sudden desire for learning, but this resolution had not lasted. It had occurred to Kitty, as she poured over yet another heavy tome, that the viscount did not seem to care about the knowledge a lady possessed. If he had been attracted to Millie, who never opened a book if she could possibly avoid it, then it was obvious that there were different things about women that appealed to him.

Her reading, therefore, was devoted to popular fiction. After all, she told himself, learning about the ways of grownup men and women would be far more useful to her than knowing the dates of wars, and the exact population of Jamaica. But sometimes she had to laugh out loud when she pictured herself holding Lionel Eden at bay while she said as passionately as the heroine in her current novel, "Desist, sir! Know that I am not to be trifled with!"

It was especially ridiculous when she knew there was nothing she would like more than to be trifled with by her dear Lion.

The Cahills arrived in Berkeley Square one afternoon in late April. They were just in time to celebrate Lady Catherine's fifteenth birthday with an excursion to the theater early the following week. And it was not very long before they were swept up in all the activities that comprised the London Season. There was a great deal of shopping to do, gowns to be ordered and accessories found, as well as calls made on all the family and any old friends of Lady Deane's who might be relied on to include Lady Millicent in their parties.

Lady Catherine forced herself to remain very much in the background, as befitted a young girl, but the first thing she always did was to evaluate any gentlemen they met with an eye to Millie's future. The Marquess of Warthen might be a possibility, for he was definitely attracted, she thought. But how unfortunate he was so bow-legged! She did not think even his exalted title could overcome that handicap! And Mr. King, although tall and handsome, was so very poor. Millie, she knew, intended to marry wealth, first and foremost. As for Sir Percival Flowers, his stutter made it difficult for anyone to converse with him, and Sir Ralph Booth was too old, and ugly to boot. Kitty sighed a little. Somehow she had thought she would find the metropolis strewn with handsome, wealthy peers, all waiting with the utmost impatience to whisk her sister into matrimony. But it appeared London was no different than the country, and a deeper, more careful search would have to be made.

One of the first people Lady Deane and her daughters called on, of course, was the Dowager Duchess of Wynne. She lived near them in the square with her two middle-aged companions, Miss Jane and Miss Eliza.

Lady Catherine wondered if the dowager would even remember her, as she made her demure curtsy. She looked up, however, when the dowager chuckled and said, "Kitty Cahill! My dear girl, how nicely you have grown up after all!"

Kitty smiled, remembering the rapport she had felt for this elderly woman with her fly-away hair and dimming eyesight. "I am afraid it was inevitable, ma'am," she said. "In spite of my trying to stay a child as you recommended."

Lady Deane looked a little confused, although she was delighted the dowager seemed to have taken to Kitty. She had noticed that the matriarch of the family had dismissed Millie after only a word or two. "I would not say that Kitty is all that grown up, your grace," she remarked. "She has just had her fifteenth birthday."

The dowager nodded as she motioned them to seats. "My dear Rose," she said in a voice that brooked no argument, "some women remain girls forever, and some girls become women at a startlingly young age. If I am not mistaken, your Kitty is one of the latter."

Lady Deane was not required to reply to this unfathomable remark, for the dowager turned aside just then to ask Miss Jane to order a tea tray. When she turned her attention back to her guests, she spoke to Lady Millicent.

"So, you have come to take the town by storm, have you, gel?" she asked, her faded eyes twinkling.

As Lady Millicent blushed, she added, "And so you shall. I predict a whirlwind Season, and a trip up the aisle at the end of it. You are very lovely."

"Thank you, ma'am," Millie said in her soft little

voice. "It seems like a dream come true that we are here at last!"

The dowager smiled a little, before she gave her condolences to Lady Deane on the death of her sister, which had necessitated such a long delay in her daughter's comeout.

Kitty sat on the sofa beside Lady Millicent and chatted with Miss Eliza and Miss Jane. She had liked them immediately, almost as much as she liked the dowager. There was such a merry look in their eyes, and they were so quick-witted.

Lady Deane only remained for the prescribed visiting time, and after she and her daughters had taken their leave, the dowager settled back in her wing chair and began to solicit her companions' opinion of her guests.

"Lady Deane thinks just as she ought, your grace," Miss Eliza said.

"Indeed, a most superior woman," Miss Jane agreed.

"And Lady Millicent?" the dowager asked. As they hesitated now, she laughed out loud. "I know, my dears, I know! A perfect widgeon, as simple as she is beautiful. But I foresee no problem firing her off, none at all. Now, if it had been Lady Catherine her mother was presenting this Season, we might have had to take a hand in it. Lady Catherine is not your ordinary young thing, no, indeed."

"I was surprised at how different she is from her sister in looks," Miss Jane admitted. "Is she the only one in the family with that startling red hair?"

The dowager nodded. "I was much struck with it when she leaned forward and the sun touched it," she said. "It looked like fire, did it not? However, it is nothing but a wild mane, and it needs a good crop. Something must be done about her pale eyebrows, as well."

Miss Eliza seemed confused. "But, your grace," she said, "it is the other one who is making her comeout. Lady Catherine is only fifteen."

"I was thinking ahead," the dowager admitted as she rose and gathered her shawl around her. As she did so, she knocked over a small Meissen figurine that had been placed on the table beside her. "And I do not think it is too soon to begin preparing for her future," she continued as Miss Jane righted the bibelot. "I shall suggest a good hairdresser to Lady Deane, even though we do have some time left and Lady Millicent must be fired off first."

As she made her way down the room, her two companions collectively held their breath. The dowager was noted for her awkwardness, the result of her poor eyesight. This time, however, she managed to maneuver the room without further contretemps. At the door, she turned and said, "Do me the kindness of finding out exactly when Lionel Eden, Viscount Benning, is expected to return to England, will you, my dears? Surely his Uncle Eden must be recovered by now!"

As the two middle-aged ladies smiled and nodded, she beamed at them. "Dear Jane and dear Eliza," she murmured. "I do not know what I would do without you, indeed, I don't!"

It did not take the two ladies very long to discover that the viscount planned to return home by the end of June—in fact, a single morning call on the family's premier gossip had been enough to ascertain his plans. As the two strolled back to Berkeley Square, they pondered the dowager's sudden interest in the viscount.

"Can it be that Agatha has him in mind for the lovely Lady Millicent?" Miss Eliza asked as they waited for a hackney to pass so they could cross the street.

"I don't think so," Miss Jane said slowly. "She is very fond of Lionel Eden, if you recall, dear. And I doubt she would subject him to a lifetime spent with a bubblehead."

As the two proceeded, arm in arm, she added, "I suspect it was Lady Catherine she had in mind. After all, the viscount is still a very young man, and she will not be fifteen forever!''

"I do hope we can do something to help, Jane," Miss Eliza confided. ''Things will be sadly flat now that Earl Norwell and his countess have agreed to stop disagreeing and admit they love each other.''

What Lady Deane thought of the dowager's sudden interest in her youngest daughter, she kept to herself. She had been startled to receive a note from her, ordering her to take Kitty to the best hairdresser in London. For a moment, she had felt resentment at being instructed in her own family's affairs, but she had come to see it was only typical of the dowager. She had insisted on having a finger in everyone else's pie for years, and since no one dared to refuse her assistance, she had come to expect obedience from young and old. After all, as she had told many and many a family member, she did it for their own good.

Lady Catherine was taken, therefore, to a Monsieur LeBanc, who, although he exclaimed over the color of her hair, looked a trifle tight-lipped as he set to work. His round face brightened, however, when he discovered that once his client's hair had been thinned and cut a great deal shorter, it had a natural tendency to curl. When she left the shop an hour later, Kitty's head felt pounds lighter. Her hair was now a mass of fiery ringlets that showed off her long, slim neck, and she knew that, besides being attractive, the new style made her look older.

The dowager asked her to call one morning shortly thereafter, and since Lady Deane was taking Millie for a fitting on some new gowns, Kitty walked the short distance to the dowager's imposing town house, attended only by the footman her mother insisted she take with her in London.

As she stepped into the morning room, the dowager motioned her closer, peering at her as she did so.

"Oh, excellent, my dear Kitty!" she enthused. "Turn around so I can see the back."

Kitty pirouetted and ended with a curtsy, her head tipped to one side. "I am very nice, don't you think so, ma'am?" she asked, her big green eyes twinkling.

"Very nice, indeed. I am so glad you have such lovely, clear skin. Freckles would be impossible, and yet many with your coloring are afflicted with them," said her grace, patting the seat beside her.

"Mama has always insisted on bonnets and lotions, ma'am. No freckle would dare!" Kitty said, chuckling a little as she sat down.

The dowager smiled as she rang the bell at her side. In only a few moments, her companions bustled in carrying a small wooden box and a large hand mirror. They both exclaimed over Kitty's new hairdo until the dowager said, "Yes, it is a vast improvement. And we have something here that will further improve your looks, dear girl."

She held out her hand, and Miss Jane opened the box and gave it to her. Kitty looked a little confused as the dowager took out what looked like a fat pencil.

"Let me show you," she said. "But stay! Perhaps I had better let Jane or Eliza apply the pencil. With my wretched eyesight, you might end up looking like a clown!"

As Kitty's brows rose, she added, "No, no, you must keep very still now."

Kitty was surprised when the dowager's middle-aged companion began to brush her brows with little, feathery strokes, all the while instructed by her grace. "Not too heavy, now, Eliza," she said. "It must be very subtle."

When Miss Eliza stepped back, both the dowager and Miss Jane clapped their hands. "What a difference it makes!" Miss Jane marveled. "I would never have believed it!"

The dowager handed Kitty the mirror. "You may

look now, Kitty," she said. Wide-eyed, Kitty stared at her reflection. Her pale, sandy brows had been darkened slightly, and she was amazed how this had changed her face, giving definition to what she had always considered a bland, egglike countenance.

"But—but that is a cosmetic, and nice young ladies don't paint," she whispered, horrified. As she was turning this way and that in admiration, no one took her objection at all seriously.

"So it is, but no one need know anything about it but the four of us," the dowager said firmly.

"But my mama . . ." Kitty began.

"Your mama will say nothing," the dowager interrupted. "And if by any chance she does, you just refer her to me. Now, Kitty, you must wear the pencil every day until it becomes quite an ordinary part of your appearance. And when you are a little older, and attending evening affairs, we shall see about some color for your lashes, too. They are very pale, although I see how thick they are. Of course there is no need to do anything about your cheeks or your lips. We have no intention of turning you into a common actress, my dear."

Kitty put the mirror down and looked straight at the dowager. "Why are you helping me so much, your grace?" she asked. And then, as if she felt that statement too bald and unappreciative, she added quickly, "Not that I am not delighted, of course!"

"Because I like you," the dowager replied. "You are a very attractive girl with that fiery red hair and lovely skin. But even Mother Nature needs a discreet helping hand, every now and again.

"Besides, if you begin now, at fifteen, by the time you make your comeout, your darker brows will be an accepted part of you. But you must practice the application carefully, Kitty, and acquire a light, deft touch!"

Kitty nodded, and accepted the little box Miss Eliza

pressed into her hands, winking as she did so. Seeing she still looked a little doubtful, the dowager added, "Women have been using artifices for centuries, my dear. Sometimes it is a discreet bit of padding, or a tightly laced corset if they have the opposite problem. Little women wear higher heels, and tall ladies, flat sandals. And why do you think women visit hair-dressers, and fuss so over their ensembles, if not out of concern for their appearance? My dear child, I am sure Eve herself discovered what some of the berries in the Garden of Eden could do to improve her looks, and remember, she did not even have any competition for Adam!"

Kitty laughed out loud then, amused and reassured, and she could not resist giving her hostess a hug before they all settled down for a comfortable visit.

"Lady Millicent is enjoying her stay in London?" the dowager asked.

"Oh, she is as merry as a grig," Kitty told her. "However, I must admit I am disappointed in town."

"Indeed?" the dowager prodded as her young guest frowned a little. "In what way?"

Kitty's frown deepened. "I had thought the gentle-men would be more impressive," she admitted. "You see, it is of the utmost importance that Millie marries without delay, and I have found no one suitable as yet. They are either poor, old, ugly, or afflicted with some terrible handicap—bow legs or a stutter. It is too bad!"

None of the audience that was listening so closely was so gauche as to inquire why Lady Catherine felt she must take a direct hand in her sister's future, when Lady Millicent had a perfectly capable mother to see to it.

Instead, they murmured their agreement and Kitty clasped her hands together tightly in her lap as she added, "I do not know how much time I have, so I must make haste!"

The dowager patted her hands. "If you would care for it, Kitty, we shall be glad to assist you. And I think you might very well agree that with my dear Jane and Eliza on the job, the problem of Lady Millicent's intended is as good as solved. Is that not so, my dears?''

Her two companions tittered and blushed, as Kitty looked wondering from one to the other. She was further surprised to see Miss Jane take a pad and pencil from the sewing basket at her feet and begin a list as the dowager questioned Kitty about the type of husband her sister might prefer.

For the next half hour, Kitty listened carefully, as first one, and then another gentleman were introduced as a prospect, and his strengths and weaknesses discussed in a most explicit, straightforward way.

At last the dowager nodded. "Yes, either Sir John Phillips or Lord Bertram Fitton will do very well, very well, indeed. And although, I, myself, prefer Bertie for the position—such a dear, undemanding man he is!— we will allow Lady Millicent to make the final decision.

"Now, I think we had better see about putting them in her way without further delay. In fact, I shall give a dinner party and small dance in a week's time, and include them on the guest list. And I really do not think you need worry that curly red head of yours a moment longer, my dear Kitty."

A little while later, Lady Catherine Cahill walked home with a light step, smiling to herself as she did so. Whoever would have thought the Dowager Duchess of Wynne would make such a wonderful friend and ally? And Miss Jane and Miss Eliza, too! And they had not even bothered to ask why Millie's marriage was so important to her, and for that she was very grateful. She could not tell them of her love for the viscount; she could not share that with anyone!

A young gentleman approaching from the opposite direction touched his hat to her and bowed slightly, smiling at her as he did so. He seemed about to speak to her until her footman drew closer and coughed a little behind his glove. A rueful expression crossed the stranger's face as Kitty sailed by him with her head held high. She was barely able to contain her giggles at his admiration, and she was sure the reason he had even noticed her was directly related to the little wooden box tucked in her reticule, for no one had ever honored her this way before.

Later, at dinner, Millie told her she had never realized she had such a pretty sister. Kitty held her breath, but Millie only added that her new hair style made such a difference in her looks, it was hard to believe.

Kitty did see her mother studying her carefully, but she did not comment on any change in her appearance. She noticed, however, that Lady Deane made a morning call on the dowager the very next day, and she went alone. She was gone for a very long time, and when she returned, she made no mention of her call, nor what had transpired during it.

Not another word was said about Lady Catherine's discreetly darkened eyebrows, although sometimes, in the days that followed, she wondered why her mama seemed to stare at her so often, and why, as she did so, her expression was so bemused and somehow disbelieving.

Five

T HE EVENING OF the dowager duchess's dinner party and dance duly arrived, and Lady Catherine waved her mother and sister on their way with a warm smile. She, herself, intended to spend the evening with a good book. She had discovered the circulating libraries in London by this time, and she was delighted at the whole new world of romance they opened for her. Her present book, written by "An Unknown Lady," was vastly entertaining, even a little naughty. She was glad her mama had so little time to inspect her selections now they had come to town, for if she had, Kitty knew she would have taken the book away from her at once. But the lovely, although a trifle dim-witted, heroine, was having such an exciting time of it, pursued as she was by the most mesmeric, dangerous villain Kitty had ever imagined. She was not concerned for the girl, however. She had read enough contemporary fiction to know that the equally dim-witted, albeit handsome, hero would rescue her before the villain could succeed in his plan to seduce her.

The next morning, sounding almost surprised, Millie told her all about the party, and how much she had enjoyed it. She had anticipated a dull, dry evening, for the dowager was so old, and so forbidding, she told her intently interested sister as they sat together at breakfast. But to her amazement, there had been several young people there, including a pair of handsome gentlemen who had been most attractive. Even Mama had been pleased to see how taken a Sir John Phillips—tall and dark—and Lord Bertram Fitton—equally tall, with wavy blond hair—had been. When the butler knocked and came in to present her with two bouquets, Millie blushed and smiled. Silently and fervently, Lady Catherine thanked her very good friend, the dowager.

Lady Millicent was very busy in the days that followed. There were drives and walks in the park, and shopping trips, as well as expeditions to Richmond and Kew to fill her days. And in the evenings, she and her mother were seldom home, for the invitations poured in to theater parties, trips by water to Vauxhall, balls, ridottos, soirees—even a gay masquerade.

Lady Deane could only be pleased that the Dowager Duchess of Wynne took her younger daughter under her wing, for she herself did not have time to see to Kitty now. And although she still could not believe what the dowager had told her the morning she had called on her alone, she knew Kitty was as safe in her company as she would have been in her own. So Lady Catherine began to enjoy some amusements, too: drives in the dowager's landau, tea parties, and trips to the theater and opera. They spent an afternoon at the Royal Enclosure inspecting the wild animals there, and went to a performance at Astley's Amphitheater. As they drove home, Kitty apologized to the dowager for behaving like such a child, clapping much too long at the trick equestrian performance and the fearless tightrope walker. The dowager smiled and patted her hand.

"As I told you once before, dear Kitty, enjoy your childhood while you can," she said. She noticed Kitty's little frown, and she added, "Yes, yes, I know! You are not a child anymore, in fact you are well on your way to becoming a young lady, but you must never lose your zest for living. Look at me! I am scores of years older than you are, yet I enjoyed the performance as much as you did. Perhaps even more!"

Relieved, Kitty smiled again, and gave the dowager a big hug before she was set down in Berkeley Square.

Whenever she was with the dowager, the lady kept her up to date on Millie's progress. "I do believe she is leaning toward Bertie Fitton," she said once. "She danced with him twice last night, and Jane told me how happy she seemed. And although she went into supper with Sir John, Eliza mentioned that Bertie managed to get a place at her table as well. All is in train, my dear, and proceeds as I expected."

As well as keeping Kitty informed on Millie's affairs of the heart, the dowager also began another phase of that young lady's education. She was careful to do so in a way that Kitty would not recognize as instruction, making her points while discussing other young ladies.

As she poured Kitty a cup of tea one afternoon, she remarked, "You would not have believed how brazen Miss Rogers was last evening, my dear! Why, she made a dead set at your brother Emery, and that is no way to interest a gentleman, no, indeed! For even if you are mad with love, you must be subtle about it. Alas, that Miss Rogers informed the whole world of her intent, wearing her heart on her sleeve. It came as no surprise to me when Emery beat a more than hasty retreat. I could have told the girl she would have piqued his interest more by pretending to be aloof and disinterested. Then Emery might well have pursued her, to discover what there was about him that Miss Rogers could not like. But there, some girls do not even have the sense of a goose, which is to say, none at all, more's the pity."

Kitty nodded as she filed the information away, which the dowager had most certainly intended she do.

Driving in the park one afternoon, she pointed out a pretty brunette, and sighed. "That is Lady Buckley's daughter. I fear she will always be a spinster, even as lovely as she is. It is too bad!"

"Why won't she marry, your grace?" Kitty asked.

"She has never taken the time to learn the art of

conversation, and so has earned the reputation of being a bore," the dowager told her. "You see, she feels gay banter is unbecoming for a lady, so she never makes a joke or indulges in flirtation. Being so very proper, she is often left to her own devices."

"You really think she should *flirt,* ma'am?" Kitty asked, her green eyes wide.

The dowager nodded so vigorously, two hairpins went flying. "But of course! Besides being the most delightful pastime in the world, there is no harm in it. And if it is done lightly, no one connects it with pursuit."

"How does one go about learning how to flirt?" Kitty asked, frowning a little now in her concentration.

The dowager chuckled and patted her hand. "I shall tell you, my dear, not that you will have need of the art for some time. You must learn to smile in a certain, mysterious way, as if you knew a wonderful secret. Then you lower your eyes as if the gentleman you have just met is too wonderful to contemplate for more than a second at a time. Watch your sister—she is an expert! And you must say something to keep the man's interest. It is best if you can find out something about him before you meet, so you will know in advance what will keep him at your side. Is he mad for horses? Compliment him on his team! Is he a sportsman? Tell him how strong he is! Is he a *gallant,* a rake? Intrigue him with the plot of a new love story, blushing a little as you do so! Oh, there are so many ways, Kitty! So many delectable, artful ways to fire his interest in you, and you, alone. And then, when he appears to be cotched, you disappear!"

"Disappear?" Kitty echoed, leaning closer in her interest.

The dowager nodded. "Let him see you in some other man's company. Let him observe how that gentleman laughs with you, asks you to dance, shows his interest. He will be at your side again before the cat has time to lick her ear!"

Kitty did not laugh at her cant, indeed, she was sighing now. "But to do that, you would have to be beautiful, otherwise it would not work at all," she said sadly.

"Nonsense!" the dowager said with a snort. "A clever woman can make any man think she is the most ravishing thing he has ever seen."

She saw Kitty shaking her head in disagreement, and she slapped her hand lightly. "Attend me well, Kitty, if you please! I was never a beauty, never. I was too tall and awkward, and much too outspoken. But I was a great flirt, for all that. And the duke proposed to me only a week after we met, much to his mother's dismay. She had chosen a winsome little blonde for him, but my dear Reggie would have none of her."

The dowager smiled, lost in memory. "What a wonderful marriage we had, Kitty! Indeed, I miss him still every day, and it has been years since he was taken from me. I pray you will know that joy too, my dear. I am sure you will."

And then, remembering Kitty's earlier comment, she added, "Besides, you are far from being a mean bit. Why, your figure is elegant, and you are very graceful as well. And with your stunning hair, you outshine a great many other young ladies."

Kitty made a *moué* of distaste. "But I have this horrid, boring face, and these ugly eyes. I know I look just like a cat."

The dowager stared at her. "You are all about in your head, Kitty! You should be glad of your eyes, for they are unique and memorable. The eyes are the mirror of the soul, my dear, and yours shine so with spirit and intelligence. I have always been struck by them."

Just then a gentleman on horseback reined in beside them and bowed over his saddle. As the dowager ordered her coachman to stop, Kitty saw that it was Garth Allendon. She had not seen him for some time, and he appeared very much the young beau about town in his form-fitting hacking jacket and breeches, and shining high boots from Hoby.

"Your humble servant, Grandmother," he said, bowing to the dowager. Turning to Kitty, he bowed again. "And Lady Catherine. I did not know you were in town."

"Give you good day, Garth my dear," the dowager said. "Kitty is here with her family, and has been kind enough to indulge an old woman with her company. But can it be that your father has let you loose in London, *alone*? And you only nineteen, too? Tsk! Tsk!"

Kitty saw a flush creep up above Garth Allendon's collar, and for a moment, she almost pitied him in his embarrassment. That is, she did until she remembered what a misery he had always made her life whenever she visited Wynne.

"I came up to town with m'father this morning, Grandmother," he managed to get out, sounding more than a little choked. "He will be calling on you tomorrow."

"Oh, that's all right, then," the dowager said, smiling now. "I take it Marjorie remained at Wynne?"

"Mother is to join us in a week or so," he told her.

"No doubt those overgrown mops of hers needed her attention." The dowager sniffed. "We shall not keep you, Garth. Run along now, and come and see me soon, dear boy."

The marquess tipped his hat, looking black at being called a boy. Kitty stifled a giggles. He was not so very old, and he looked even younger when he blushed and scowled. She must remember that, herself. She was surprised when his eyes lingered on her face, and to practice, she tried a warm, mysterious smile. To her further surprise, his flush deepened before he rode away.

"Yes, he is terribly silly, but I have great hopes he will outgrow it," his fond grandmother said. "I do so hope his father keeps a close eye on him, however, until that happy time. Young men are the most foolish things imaginable!"

"Perhaps you should keep an eye on him as well, ma'am?" Kitty suggested.

"Have no fear, I shall," the dowager said. "It is, however, difficult for me to do so, and I do not care to estrange him. You could see how he did not care for my questions, or my suggestions. But someday, when he is mature, he will overcome his dislike for me. It was ever thus. Boys are very jealous of their consequence when they first reach manhood. And, of course, he thinks himself quite the pink of the *ton,* ripe for every rig and row in town. He is a veritable baby, and the only thing he is ripe for, is plucking by some Captain Sharp. I must remember to remind the duke of it."

Kitty sat quietly, pondering the dowager's words as they left the park. Just before they reached the Cahill town house, she asked, "But if you consider Garth very young, I must be a baby indeed, ma'am."

The dowager looked amazed. "Of course you are not, my dear. Females are always much older than males, and you were mature in your cradle. No, no! At fifteen, you are equal to any man of—oh, let us say, even twenty-three."

As the landau had stopped then, Kitty was not required to answer. But as she took her leave of the dowager, and tripped up the front steps to wave goodbye as she waited for the butler to open the door, she did not even have to wonder why her heart felt so light. Lion was twenty-three now, and the dowager had said she was his equal. Could anything be better?

But as much as she longed for him to return, she still prayed he would not do so until Millie was safely, and finally, engaged. Kitty wished she would get on with it, for it all seemed to be taking a very long time.

Kitty was not to know that Lady Millicent was enjoying her new popularity and power too much to give it up quite so soon. And although she was definitely drawn to

Lord Fitton and fully intended to marry him, she saw no
reason why she should curtail her freedom a moment
before she had to. M'lord had proposed to her twice
now, something she was careful to keep from her mama
and her sister. Each time she had told him it was too
soon, smiling wistfully as she did so, so he would not
become discouraged. She had even allowed him to kiss
and caress her at the masquerade, lest his interest flag.
No, Lady Millicent knew that dear Bertie was her future
husband, but she would let him know it in her own good
time. Why, next week Sir John was to take her to a
Venetian breakfast! She was reluctant to lose his escort
and regard, for Sir John prided himself on his resemblance to the poet Byron, and modeled himself on his
hero. He affected dark, brooding looks and enigmatic
silences, and his burning eyes made her proud of her
power over him. But even Lady Millicent could see that
a lifetime spent with a difficult gentleman prone to
dismal fits of depression, would not be the most
pleasant future she could have.

However, all unknowing of her sister's plans, Kitty
was concerned. She had no idea when the viscount
would come back from Jamaica, but no matter how
often she told herself she was being silly to worry about
it, when he was probably still in residence there, she
could not help it. For all she knew, his ship might be
dropping anchor in Plymouth harbor right now, or even
worse, he might be entering his rooms in town. She
shivered.

The dowager also was becoming impatient at the
amount of time it was taking the lovely ninny who was
Lady Millicent, to make up her mind. One afternoon, as
Kitty helped her to her carriage after she had come to
take tea with the Cahills, she said, "What a delightful
spring this has been, my dear! I cannot remember being
so amused, for which I have you to thank, puss. I do so
hope Lionel won't miss all the fun!"

"Viscount Benning?" Kitty prodded, hoping her shortness of breath would go unnoticed.

"The very one," the dowager told her, pausing before climbing into her carriage. "Eliza told me he is expected here sometime in June, so we must hope he comes sooner, not later. Good-bye, my dear. I shall see you soon, I hope."

Kitty smiled and nodded, but her mind was in turmoil. He was coming at last—he was! She went back into the house deep in thought. She could wait no longer. She must do something, and at once, to speed Millie's decision. But what on earth could she do?

She spent the evening alone in the library, going over first one plan and then another, before she discarded them all. Most of those that occurred to her were taken directly from her novels, and she could see after only a few moments thought that they were much too improbable, too wild. No, it must be something simpler, she thought. She propped her chin up on one hand and stared unseeing into the dark hearth. She was almost positive that it was Lord Fitton her sister admired the most. Certainly she spoke of him more often, and it was only his bouquets that adorned her dressing table. Not that she was not attracted to Sir John Phillips, of course, but Kitty thought she was drawn to him in the same way a moth is drawn to a flame. Besides, she herself had seen enough of that young man to know he would make a miserable husband for her sunny-tempered older sister. It must be Lord Fitton. Now, how do I get him to propose? she wondered. And soon, too?

She reviewed everything she knew of Millie. She was not a complicated person, but she did like romance and intrigue. Perhaps if Lord Fitton was more romantic? That might work, she told herself, smiling a little. But how could she let him know that some fervor was required? She could hardly walk up to him and baldly suggest it.

Lady Catherine frowned. Perhaps she should ask the
dowager? Surely she would know the best way to go
about it, and since she had offered to help, as had Miss
Jane and Miss Eliza, Kitty did not think they would let
her down now. Having reached this momentous
decision, she took herself off to bed. She knew the
dowager was engaged with friends the following
morning, but she would run around the square to her
town house later in the day.

As it turned out, she was able to manage the thing by
herself after all. She was in the drawing room when she
heard Lord Fitton in the hall the following afternoon.
Millie and Lady Deane had gone out, and Lady
Catherine was alone. Taking a deep breath, she ran out
just as the butler was telling m'lord that the lady he had
come to see was not at home.

"Why, there you are, Lord Fitton," Kitty said with a
smile. "Won't you come in and wait for Millie? She and
Mama were only going on a short errand; they should be
home soon."

As the butler frowned at her, she waved her hand in
dismissal. "It will be quite all right, Biggars. You shall
bring m'lord a glass of wine, and I shall entertain him."

Glad of the opportunity, Lord Fitton bowed to her.
"How kind of you, Lady Catherine! I should be delighted."

He followed her back to the drawing room, leaving
the butler to shake his head at the girl's forward ways.
But Biggars had known Lady Catherine from childhood, and he thought of her as little more than a child
now. Surely, at her age, there could be no impropriety
in her entertaining her sister's beau.

Kitty had spoken to Lord Fitton many times before,
in the course of his courtship of Lady Millicent. Sometimes Kitty had even entertained him as she was doing
now, while he waited for Millie to decide which bonnet
she wished to wear.

Lord Fitton found Lady Catherine agreeable,

although he wondered that two sisters could be so disparate. Lady Catherine was frank and outspoken, where Millie was all shy smiles and blushes. And she was so much more beautiful than Lady Catherine, who had that startling hair and unblinking, cat-green eyes.

He smiled at her now, however, as he took the seat she indicated. As she returned that smile, he thought her a taking little thing, in spite of her theatrical looks.

"I say she will only be a little while, but I may be wrong," Lady Catherine began as she sat down and adjusted her skirts. "Millie has trouble making up her mind, you see." She sighed a little, trying not to be obvious as she gauged m'lord's reaction to this serious failing.

Lord Fitton only smiled. He was a handsome, conventional man in his late twenties, well pleased with both himself and his world. "But of course, I understand," he told Kitty. "Most ladies are the same when it comes to their gowns and fripperies. You will be just like her in a few year's time, m'lady."

Kitty nodded, although she had no intention of ever becoming so wishy-washy. She drew a deep breath and said artlessly, "How glad I am that you came late, m'lord! Biggars was forced to send Sir John Phillips away not an hour ago, for there could be no question of his waiting for such a long time. It was too bad, for he had the most beautiful bouquet, and he appeared very eager to see Millie."

Lord Fitton frowned. So, that worthless rival of his was still persisting in his pursuit of Lady Millicent's hand, was he? He had suspected as much! He forgot himself far enough to gnaw on his thumbnail as he wondered what he could do to dispose of the man with his dark handsome looks, and poetic inclinations. It would be too bad if Millie was taken in by him!

"He is such a romantic looking man, is he not? I am sure I do not wonder that he makes Millie tremble so," Lady Catherine went on, trembling a little herself at her daring. "She told me he did," she added, fueling the fire.

"Indeed?" the viscount asked, sounding grim.

Kitty nodded, opening her eyes very wide as she continued, "Oh, yes, for Millie does so love romance! I am sure she will marry some man who is romantic to a fault."

She saw the viscount was frowning in earnest now, and she was sure he was wondering how he could suddenly change his prosaic personality into one of a dashing lover. When he did not speak, nor his expression change, she decided she would have to help him.

"We have been reading a most interesting book together," she said. "It has such an impetuous hero, why, he sweeps the heroine into his arms and kisses her until she promises to marry him without delay. How Millie sighed when she read that passage! I think she was wishing she might have such a tempestuous wooing, herself."

She saw Lord Fitton's face brighten a little, and she changed the subject before he could think to ask why the superior Lady Deane allowed her daughters to read such drivel, most especially a young lady who was not even out.

The two chatted lightly on a number of subjects from then on. Kitty was more than willing to carry more than her share of the conversation, for she could see the viscount was a trifle abstracted. When Lady Deane and Millie came in half an hour later, she rose at once to excuse herself. Her throat was hoarse from all her prattle, and she knew she would not be missed.

"Mama, would you please come up and look at my green walking gown?" she asked Lady Deane. "I am afraid the maid has scorched it near the hem, and I don't know what to do about it."

Lady Deane, who was about to take a seat and play propriety, turned and frowned. "Scorched it, Kitty? I shall come at once!"

Rose Cahill was glad of the interruption, for she herself was growing weary of Millie's vacillating. Perhaps if she left her alone with Lord Fitton things would come to a head, she thought as she made her excuses and bustled away in the wake of her younger daughter. She did not close the door completely, however, but left it several inches ajar. Even though she had decided the viscount would make a most agreeable son-in-law, there was a limit to what she would allow.

Lady Millicent barely had time to settle herself prettily on the sofa before Lord Fitton took the place beside her and drew her into his arms. This was so unlike him that Millie stared, her mouth forming a perfect "O" of astonishment. Lord Fitton did not hesitate. Bending his head and pressing her even closer, he covered her mouth with his own. His kiss was insistent and passionate, a complete change from the tentative, reverent kiss he had given her at the masquerade. Lady Millicent had been trying to push him away, but now her arms crept up around his neck, and she nestled closer as a tide of warmth spread over her body.

This was Bertie? This ardent, demanding, eager lover? When he lifted his head, it took her a moment before she could catch her breath. But when she would have scolded him, he gave her no opportunity to even begin.

"My darling Millicent!" he exclaimed, his voice unsteady, yet urgent. "Forgive me, but I could not resist you! I have waited so long, so very long, for you to say that you will be mine. And now I find I can wait no longer. Tell me you love me, my darling, as I love you! Promise me you will marry me as soon as it can be arranged!"

Millie opened her mouth to reply, but, perversely, the viscount did not allow her to answer this most important question. Instead, his lips wandered over her face and throat, covering them with kisses before they reclaimed her own. Lady Millicent was beginning to feel bewildered, even a little dizzy. And when, held tight in one strong arm, his other hand cupped her breasts and caressed them, she almost fainted.

"Bertie!" she whispered against his mouth. "Stop, oh, stop! You must not!"

"But I must," he said firmly, his breath coming quickly. "You are altogether too beautiful, too desirable! You drive me mad!"

He groaned and buried his face in her neck. Over his head, Lady Millicent heard the butler coughing in the hall, and she was recalled to her senses. The door was open and Bertie had such a loud, carrying voice! Had Biggars heard his impassioned words? Were he and the footmen even now exchanging glances or winks? Was he getting ready to march in here and adjust the drapes or offer to replenish m'lord's wine glass to ensure her purity? How embarrassing! She would not be able to bear it!

Pushing the viscount away from her, she straightened her gown, her eyes still on the drawing room door. "If you don't stop this, I shall scream!" she hissed. Her steely whisper was most unlike her usual dulcet tones, but Lord Fitton was too far gone to notice.

"I shall never stop until I have your promise, Millicent," he told her in a voice she considered much too loud. He captured her hands again and exclaimed, "Tell me you will marry me! Tell me at once!"

"Shhh!" Millicent hissed. She heard the butler's cough again, a little nearer, and in desperation, she said, "For heaven's sake, all right! I will! But if you touch me again, I won't!"

Lord Fitton smiled broadly, completely undeterred by this less than gracious reply to his proposal. As Lady Millicent pulled away from him and pointed sternly to the other end of the sofa, he nodded. No doubt he had frightened her a little, he told himself smugly. Such an innocent creature could have no idea of a man's passion when it was not merely written about in a book. But he was delighted Lady Catherine had showed him the best way to go on, for just see how it had answered! Lady Millicent had given him her promise!

"I am the happiest man in the world, my darling," he said, as she settled her skirts and smoothed her curls.

Lady Millicent had no chance to reply, and tell her intended how happy she was in turn, even if she had been so inclined, for Biggars knocked on the door then, and entered on his knock. He bowed slightly before he walked with a stately tread to the front window. Just as Millie had predicted, he made quite a show of adjusting them against the afternoon glare.

Lady Millicent took a deep breath, and began to tell m'lord about her shopping expedition, and the delightful bonnet she had seen that was such a perfect match for her new afternoon gown. Lord Fitton smiled and nodded. As the butler left the room, Lady Millicent wished Bertie would say something. For him just to sit there looking fatuous and a bit idiotic was making her nervous. Besides, she was more than a little displeased to have had her hand forced. There were several weeks left in the Season, and now, as an engaged girl, she would not be able to dance with all the handsome *beaux,* receive their calls, or look forward to their impassioned notes and pretty gifts of flowers and trinkets. It was too bad! And she had no idea how things had come to such a pass, and after all her careful planning, too!

Upstairs, Lady Catherine wondered how everything was going in the drawing room between her sister and the suddenly passionate Lord Fitton. Her conversation was a little disjointed, therefore, as she tried to explain to her mama that she had been sure the gown was scorched. However could she have been mistaken? she asked, turning the fabric slowly between her hands. Perhaps it had been a trick of the light?

Six

LIONEL EDEN, Viscount Benning, arrived in London some nine days later. The very next morning, he strolled around to Berkeley Square to pay his respects to the Dowager Duchess of Wynne.

He found her still at the breakfast table with her two middle-aged companions, and for a few minutes, there was a great deal of confusion. The dowager insisted on a hearty kiss before she ordered a fresh pot of coffee, and some breakfast for him. His protestations that he had already eaten were ignored as if he had never made them. The viscount shrugged. For some reason, the dowager wanted him to remain for awhile, and he was perfectly agreeable, for he had always admired her, especially her spirit. He saw her take Miss Jane and Miss Eliza aside and give them some quiet instructions before she took her seat at the table and beamed at him. Her two companions almost scurried in their haste to leave the room. Idly, the viscount wondered what that had been all about.

"Dear Lionel, how glad I am that you have come back at last!" the dowager exclaimed. "I take it that your Uncle Eden is well now, and has no further need of your services?"

She thought her guest's face a little grim as he said, "He is much better, ma'am, but he will never be the same as he was before the accident. Both my aunt and uncle begged me to stay and continue to run the plantation, but I said I could not decide on permanency until I had returned to England, at least for a visit.''

He frowned a little, staring down into his coffee cup as if seeking the answer to his dilemma there. The dowager studied him as he did so. She knew Lionel Eden was only twenty-three, but he had the appearance of a much more mature and exprienced man. She wondered what had happened to him in Jamaica to bring about such a change? The gay, laughing, careless Lion she had known, so adored by his family and friends, was gone, and in his stead had come this serious man, the twinkle in his eyes replaced by a watchful gleam. But as much as she wanted to question him about it, she refrained. She would find out in due course, and perhaps be able to help him reach a decision about his future, but that time was not now.

Accordingly, she amused him with stories of the *ton* and the Season, gave him the latest family news, and inquired after his parents, while the viscount discovered he was hungry after all. As the dowager chatted, he tucked into the sirloin and shirred eggs, the scones and strawberry preserves, with a will.

''My mother and father are both well, ma'am, and send their regards. I went to Sutherland Hall first, of course, before coming to town. But my father insisted I come up to London before the Season was over, and to tell truth, I was not loath to do so. I feel the need for some gaiety and amusement after my long exile.''

''Is that how you think of Jamaica, Lionel?'' the dowager asked. ''As a place of exile?''

He stopped cutting his beef, an arrested expression on his handsome face. ''It is, when you are not free to leave, your grace,'' he said. ''Strange, that. I never considered it that way before, but these past three years have been long and hard.''

The dowager was not able to comment, for there was a knock on the door then. She looked up expectantly to see Lady Catherine running in, swinging her bonnet by its ribbons. The girl stopped suddenly, her eyes widening. The note that Miss Jane had sent across the square so hurriedly had not mentioned the viscount, and she had had no idea she was to come face to face with him.

And then, after a heart-stopping moment, she ran forward, her arms outstretched. "Lion!" she cried, her eyes glowing with her delight. "Is it you? Is it *really* you at last?"

The viscount rose to his feet, wiping his mouth on his napkin as he did so. His dark blue eyes twinkled in quite the old way as he bowed. "Well, here's a pretty welcome," he said. "And a quite unexpected one, too."

Lady Catherine stopped in her tracks. She made herself take a deep breath. How impulsive and young she must seem to him, running toward him and exclaiming! she thought.

"You must forgive me, m'lord," she said, slowing her speech and trying desperately to steady her voice. "It was just that you have been gone for such a long time, and I did not expect to see you." She dropped him a curtsy and said, "Welcome home, m'lord. I trust you had a pleasant journey?"

The dowager smiled to herself as she said, "Come and sit down and have some coffee, Kitty. I quite forgot in the excitement of Lionel's arrival that we were to drive out this morning, but I know you will forgive me."

Lady Catherine took her place opposite the viscount, and tried hard not to stare at him. She knew she had no appointment with the dowager this morning, but she was more than happy to continue the charade, and delighted that she had been summoned.

After a moment, she dared to look at Lionel Eden again. He was staring at her, and she blushed and lowered her eyes, remembering to smile a little as she did so.

"But what a change these past three years have made

in you, m'lady!" he said. "I see my little Miss Kittycat is forever gone. I would mourn her passing if this stunning, grownup lady that I see before me had not taken her place, indeed, I would."

Lady Catherine made herself laugh, even though she had heard the teasing note in his voice and interpreted it correctly. "If you remember, m'lord, I told you I would grow up just as fast as I could, did I not?"

Slowly, Lionel Eden lowered his coffee cup. He had suddenly been reminded of a cold January morning when he had stood on the steps of Wynne, while the child that used to be his Miss Kittycat had begged him to wait for her because she loved him. But surely she was not referring to that! he thought. It could only embarrass her to recall how frank she had been, declaring her love. Now, of course, she must realize it had only been a child's infatuation.

"I remember," he said, "even though it was a long time ago. But I have been most remiss! Do tell me how Aunt Rose and Uncle Reginald are, and my good friend Emery? And give me news of Lady Millicent, if you would be so good."

Lady Catherine was delighted to begin with the latter. "Millie has just become engaged to Lord Bertram Fitton, m'lord," she said, trying not to sound overjoyed that it was so. She peeked at him, but she could not tell by his expression whether he was sorry or not. Thank heavens she had been able to bring it about! she thought as he nodded. She told him then that Emery was expected in town any day, and added that he and her parents would be delighted to welcome him.

"I shall make it a point to call," he said. "For of course I must offer my best wishes to the beautiful Lady Millicent. Lord Fitton is a lucky man."

"Oh, it ended up being quite the whirlwind affair," the dowager interjected. "From what I have learned, he quite swept her off her feet. Isn't that so, puss?"

Lady Catherine and the dowager exchanged smiles,

and Viscount Benning wondered what secrets they shared. If ever he had seen two conspirators! They seemed an incongruous pair, the tall, elderly gray-haired matriarch and the slim young girl with the flaming hair and big green eyes, but he could tell they were the best of friends. How old was Lady Catherine now? he wondered. He was twenty-three, so that must make her sixteen? No, fifteen. Strange, she seemed much older than that, somehow. He studied her delicate profile and long slender neck, those fiery, shining curls.

His eyes went beyond her then to admire the pleasant breakfast room. The spring sunlight was streaming in through the long windows that faced the garden. Beyond those windows, he could see pale green new leaves and well-raked gravel paths. Some bright flowers made a bold display, dancing a little in the breeze. It was a cool, fresh morning, the kind he had dreamed of for such a long time. How he had missed England with its change of seasons, so ordered and yet so varied! In Jamaica the weather was almost always the same, one warm, bright day following another, except during the rainy season. He remembered even thinking with longing of a thick, dank fog, when the lushness of the mountainous terrain palled after a few months.

Last Christmas he had felt an ache in his chest, he was missing the cold and snow of home so, and he had envied everyone in the family who was celebrating the holiday season at Wynne. And then he had set himself to admire the sweet scent of the tropical flowers, the little trade wind that stirred the draperies of the dining salon, as he tried to pretend to his aunt and uncle that he was well content to be with them. He felt he had been living a lie for years.

He remembered now, one lonely evening two months ago, he had picked up a book of Shakespeare's plays. He had riffled through it until his eye was caught by a passage in *Richard II* that had decided the matter for him, once and for all. It was that familiar speech by

King Richard's uncle, the Duke of Lancaster, about his country, and as he read the words, Lionel Eden's mouth twisted almost in pain. "This little world, set in a silver sea . . . this blessed plot, this earth, this realm, this England . . . this dear, dear land." And it was then, as he felt tears prickling his eyelids, that he had known he must come home.

He was recalled to his surroundings now as the dowager asked if he would care for more coffee. He smiled and shook his head. "Thank you, but no, your grace. I must be on my way, for I have an appointment in the city."

As he spoke, he rose and bowed. "But I do thank you for the wonderful English breakfast. It made me feel I am really home at last. Lady Catherine, your servant," he added, bowing to Kitty now.

She rose from her chair and curtsied, "I shall tell my mother and father of your return, m'lord," she said, those wide green eyes never leaving his. "They will be so glad to see you again!"

She stood staring after him until the door closed behind him, and then she took her seat again. The dowager was deep in her post now, or at least she was pretending to be, and Kitty stared at the viscount's empty chair, dreaming a little.

Lion was different, and she was not sure she liked the change. He was much less mercurial, and his wonderful, flashing smile was often absent. Indeed, she had seen a strained look in his eyes more than once, and she had wanted to run to him and insist he tell her what was troubling him. She still felt breathless from her first sight of him, after all this time, but she did not think he had noticed, or the dowager either. But how her heart had leapt in her breast when she saw him there, so tall and handsome, his auburn hair streaked with golden highlights, and his skin bronzed dark by the southern sun. Kitty nodded to herself. She knew she had made no mistake those three years ago. Lionel Eden was the man

—the only man—for her. And now that she was almost grown, surely he would see that she was the woman he must have at his side, too.

She frowned then. She was not a woman. She was just turned fifteen, and there were still years to go before he would think of her that way. Why, even his teasing remark that Miss Kittycat was no more, had been made lightly, almost in jest. Kitty stared down at her slender body. True, she was taller, as tall as Millie now, but her figure was still immature. And, she suspected, it would never sport the rich curves of her sister and the other Incomparables. It was sad, but there was nothing she could do about it. But at least her face had more definition now, and she knew her horrid red hair was arranged in a becoming style. Well, she would not despair, she told herself, nodding a little as she did so. Lionel Eden was worth her most monumental effort.

She felt the dowager's gaze, and she turned to her, her green eyes locking with her friend's.

"Shall we go for a drive, Kitty?" the old lady asked. "It will make my lie truth after all."

"You know, don't you?" Kitty asked, getting right to the heart of her problem.

The dowager nodded. "Oh, I have known this age, puss. I did think perhaps it was only a passing thing, and one that would soon be forgotten. But this morning it was obvious from your face that it has not been. And that is why I did not have Jane warn you that Lionel was here. I wanted to see for myself if your affection for him was real.

"But Kitty, you are indeed unique. Girlish infatuations, even first love, rarely last. But you have not wavered in your resolve even though he has been absent for three years. Why, you remind me of the hero of Sir Walter Scott's *Marmion*! I shall have to call you *Lady Lochinvar*!"

Seeing Kitty looked puzzled, she said, "Surely you remember the poem, my dear? The young lord who rode

out of the west, who was so faithful in love and
dauntless in war?''

As Kitty smiled and nodded, she added, "You have
certainly been faithful, and dauntless as well. It is truly
astounding! Of course a great deal of time must elapse
before we can do anything about it. . . .''

Her voice trailed away. As she rose, Kitty went to
help her. "I know," she said, trying to keep the despair
from her voice. "That is what worries me the most,
ma'am. What if he falls in love with someone else
before I am old enough? And all I know how to do is
pray hard that he will not.''

"And of course Lionel is the reason you had to get
Lady Millicent engaged so quickly, is that not so?'' the
dowager asked as the two of them walked arm and arm
to the door.

Kitty nodded. "Yes, he was attracted to her at Wynne
the last time we were there together. I was afraid that
attraction might be rekindled now. But even with Millie
safely betrothed, there are other girls—beautiful,
wealthy, accomplished, voluptuous, *fascinating* girls!
And all of them will want him, even as I do. It—it is a
terrible problem!''

The dowager patted the hand nearest her. "Lionel is
very young still, Kitty, in spite of his startling air of
maturity and experience. I do not expect him to consider
matrimony for some time. Most men do not, unless they
are forced to it, as I know very well. And you may be
sure I shall not urge Lionel Eden to take himself a wife,
even to solve whatever problem is bedeviling him.''

The dowager thought long and hard the next few
days. She was trying to find a way to get Viscount
Benning and Lady Catherine together without being
obvious about it and arousing his suspicions. But since
the young lady was not out, and could not attend *ton*
parties, or balls, there was little that she could do. She

did manage to suggest to him one evening at the Earl and Countess of Norwell's soiree that Kitty was pining, left alone as much as she was. The viscount commended her for her concern, and told her how good she was to see to the girl's amusement, before he went off to dance with what the dowager considered a truly insipid brunette.

She had heard from Lady Catherine that she had met the viscount a few times while riding in the park with her brother, Emery, and that he had joined them with every sign of delight. But Kitty also had to admit, honest as she had always been, that most of the conversation concerned horseflesh, cockfights, and the results of the latest meeting at Newmarket. Kitty had not tried to interrupt this masculine chitchat. Emery suffered her company more easily, now that she was no longer a child, but she knew if she tried to join in, or called attention to herself in any way, he would be quick to banish her.

As promised, the viscount had called on the Cahills and been invited to dine. Kitty thought Millie seemed almost pensive as she studied him, and she felt a shiver from her toes to the top of her head at the danger she had circumvented with so little time to spare. Whew! she thought, as her sister gave the viscount her most seductive smile.

Whenever she was alone with her brother, Kitty questioned him about Lionel Eden, for they were often in each other's company.

"Does it not seem to you that the viscount has changed, Em'ry?" she asked one morning as they turned their horses for home after an early ride. "He seems different to me, somehow."

Emery Cahill frowned. "You're right, Kitty," he said. "He *is* different, but he never speaks of why that should be so. Some of the chaps have tried to question him about Jamaica, but he will never discuss it. He says he has come home to forget the place, and have a high old time." Emery Cahill laughed then. "And so he is, my, yes! A very high old time of it!"

He turned a little then, to see his sister's wide green eyes staring at him in consideration, and he flushed. He knew very well it was not at all proper to discuss such things with a young girl, and he was quick to change the subject. Blond opera dancers or high-priced brothels, all-night gambling parties and other bachelor revels should in no way be a part of Kitty's education.

If Emery had but known it, Kitty was well aware of her dear Lion's activities, for the dowager had set Miss Jane and Miss Eliza to ferreting out information about him, and making a complete report. It was true that Kitty's spirits had flagged when she heard about the opera dancer, but the dowager had laughed at her.

"Better her than some prim young miss all intent on the altar, puss," she had said briskly. "It is only the way of all men. And certainly Lionel has no intention of *marrying* the chit, you know. No, indeed. As a son of the Marquess of Sutherland, he is well aware of what he owes his name."

As she was walking home after this meeting, Lady Catherine wondered what her mother would make of the dowager's revelations. No doubt she would be shocked and disapproving. Kitty, herself, had been a little surprised to be told such *outré* things, until she remembered with delight that the dowager had never treated her like a child. And, of course, she was right. Lion was much safer in a demimonde's, rather than a debutante's, embrace. Kitty hoped the opera dancer would hold his interest for a long time, and that there were others like her waiting in the wings to take her place. She giggled a little at her unconventional thoughts. To even imagine she was fervently promoting Lion's involvement with any other woman but herself was absurd.

She was driving in Hyde Park with her mama, Millie,

and Lord Fitton one lovely afternoon when she spotted
Lion deep in conversation with a man she did not know.
This man was considerably older than the viscount, and
dressed in the height of fashion. Kitty saw him put his
hand on Lion's arm, and bend closer to whisper in his
ear. Just before the landau swept past, she saw Lion put
his head back and laugh, in quite his old way. Kitty felt
a pang of jealousy that this older, unknown man could
amuse her viscount so.

She saw him with the viscount again late the following
morning. She had gone out for a walk with her maid,
and when she saw Lionel Eden approaching from the
opposite direction her heart leapt in that now familiar
way. Lion stopped and bowed to her, sweeping his tall
beaver from his handsome head as he did so. The gentleman who stood slightly to one side of him, raised his
quizzing glass in an intent, inch by inch perusal. Kitty
felt her cheeks grow warm.

"Good morning, Lady Catherine," the viscount said,
his wide grin at odds with his formality. "And a
beautiful morning it is, don't you agree?"

"Indeed, m'lord," Kitty said. "We have not seen you
much of late. I hope you are enjoying your stay in
London?"

"I am indeed, Miss Kittycat," he told her, grinning to
himself as he did so. Kitty was sure he was thinking of
his opera dancer, and her flush deepened. He bowed
again, and would have passed her except Kitty was
quick to put her hand on his arm.

"I hope you will call again soon, m'lord," she said.
"You have yet to tell me all your news, and I quite long
to hear it."

Since the viscount had not introduced her to the
gentleman accompanying him, she was able to ignore
his little superior smile. Now that they were close, she
could see he was only of average height, with smooth
brown hair and a thin, ordinary face. But it was his eyes

that made her wary of him. They were a curious dull
brown, and seemed almost opaque, as if he were
guarding some dark secret from the world.

"I have been very busy, m'lady," Lionel Eden was
saying now. "But one day I shall come and visit, my
promise on it."

He bowed again, and Kitty stepped aside. She knew
there was no way she could detain him further. As the
two men strolled past, she heard the stranger murmur in
an oddly light, high voice, "Cradle robbing, Lion?
Shame on you!"

What the viscount said in reply she never knew, for a
tradesman who was passing in an old cart was loudly
calling out his wares.

She asked the dowager about this strange new friend
of Lion's the next time she saw her. She was a little
disturbed when the dowager frowned, and tightened her
lips before she spoke.

"Eliza reports that Lionel has taken up with Sir Nigel
St. Edmunds," she said in a stiff voice.

"Who is he, and why do you look so black, ma'am?"
Kitty persisted.

"Sir Nigel is a man who has been on the town this
age," the dowager told her. "He is a wealthy baronet,
and although he has been careful—very careful!—to
keep his skirts clean of scandal, there has been some
talk. It is said he is an intimate of Prince Ernest, Duke
of Cumberland, and an infamous man. I, myself, have
never liked Sir Nigel, although he is everywhere
received." The dowager frowned again. "I was very
sorry to hear Lionel has become a companion of his,
even to the extent of deserting his younger cronies.
Perhaps it is the man's age and experience that attracts
him, for he himself has matured faster than others, due
to his years in Jamaica. And to be taken up by an older
man who has the reputation for great wit and sartorial
elegance, must make him feel quite the devilish rake.
But I cannot like it, puss. I cannot like at all."

Kitty could not like it either, and when she questioned her brother about the viscount's new companion, she saw him frown as hard as the dowager had. But Emery Cahill would not discuss the gentleman with his little sister, telling her in a cold, stiff voice that it was none of her business. Kitty longed to commiserate with him, he sounded so hurt that his old friend should prefer another companion.

The viscount did remember his promise and come and call one afternoon. It was a gray, misty day, but Lady Deane and Lady Millicent had gone out as planned to an afternoon loo party. When Biggars brought in the viscount's card, Kitty was delighted to think she would have him all to herself. She would have run to the hall to welcome him, until she reminded herself such behavior was childish. Instead, she asked the butler to show the viscount in, and ordered him a glass of her father's best Canary. While she waited, she smoothed her hair and her gown. If only she had known he was coming, she would not have worn this horrid old muslin! she thought.

Lionel Eden was easily persuaded to remain and chat for awhile, even though little Miss Kittycat was the only Cahill at home. He had always liked her, and he knew there was nothing wrong in being alone with her, for she was still very young, and they were, after all, distantly related.

Seven

I N NO TIME at all, the viscount was lounging back in his chair, perfectly relaxed and at home. He thought it was the excellence of Lord Deane's wine, but in reality, it was Kitty's ingenuous conversation and barely concealed delight in his company that put him at his ease.

But when she began to question him about Jamaica, he frowned and shifted in his chair. Kitty could tell he was about to change the subject, and she said quickly, "What is there about that island that you do not like, m'lord?"

"Is it that obvious?" he asked a little ruefully. She saw how intent the dark blue eyes that she had always admired were on her face.

"Very obvious," she told him. "And yet three years ago, you had no such reticence. In fact, you told me all about the island, its people and their customs. What has happened since then to change your mind about it?"

The viscount still frowned as he regarded her. She was leaning forward, her big green eyes serious. The concern in them made him relax again. This was only little Miss Kittycat, after all. He could tell her.

"When I was there before, I was a visitor," he began. "Now, however, since my uncle has been crippled in that accident at the mill, I have become the principal overseer and factor. Both my aunt and uncle depend on me to run the plantation and the mill. They take it for granted that I will do so, and have made it very clear that Golden Grove will be mine someday.''

He rose then to pace the room, and Kitty's eyes never left his tall, strong figure.

"But I know, in my heart, that I do not want to live in Jamaica. I just do not know how to tell them that, for it would disappoint them so. Perhaps it would have been different if I had been the one to emigrate there, cleared the jungle, planted the cane. And unless I am mistaken, the benign, prosperous days of the large plantations are almost over. Slavery was abolished in 1807, as well it should have been, but now it is hard to hire dependable hands to work the fields. And there is unrest among these former slaves. They are being stirred up by the Maroons." He stopped then and put his hands on his hips as he shook his head at himself. "But forgive me, m'lady, for boring you with things you cannot understand or care about."

"You are wrong, Lion," Kitty told him earnestly. "I am very interested. And of course I know about the Maroons. Aren't they the Negro slaves who retreated to the interior when Britain conquered the island from the Spaniards?"

One tawny mobile eyebrow rose as the viscount took his seat again. "You are well informed, Miss Kittycat," he drawled. As she blushed, he added, "But you are right. They are the same ones who fought so fiercely for their independence for over a century. They are quiet now, but who knows what trouble they might not stir up? If it were me, I would sell Golden Grove and return to England. But I know how my aunt and uncle love the place. It is the only home they have known for years. And they depend on me. I know I must go back, that this visit is only a pleasant interlude for me. And I do not want to go."

"But it is most unfair for you to have to, in that case," Kitty said hotly. "Surely, if you explained to them . . . if you refused . . ."

"I cannot," he said simply. "They need me too badly now. And the plantation is to be my livelihood. How else can I live well on my small inheritance? There is no place for me in England."

Kitty was thinking hard. "But you could marry an heiress," she blurted out. "That would solve all your problems."

The viscount's face brightened as he chuckled. "But how unfair to the heiress, m'lady! Don't you think she might resent being courted for her gold?"

Kitty swallowed her reply that she could not envision any girl who would not like to be courted by Lion Eden. She also put from her mind her own sizable dowry. After a moment, she said, "But you are Viscount Benning, and therefore have land here. Where is it?"

"Benning?" the viscount asked, putting down his wine glass. "Why, not far from town in the vicinity of Maidenhead, as a matter of fact. I have not seen it this age. But I know it only produces a very small income, certainly not one I could depend on for support."

"But how do you know what it can produce if you have not seen it?" Kitty persisted. "You may have the best agent in the world, but if you do not watch him, he will not put himself to any trouble or extra exertion. I think you ought to ride out there and inspect your holdings. There might be a way for you to make it more profitable. There is a manor house?"

The viscount nodded. "Yes, a lovely old manor set in pretty gardens, if I remember correctly. It is probably in a state of great disrepair, for no one has lived there for years except a pair of elderly retainers."

Lady Catherine sighed. "I would love to see it," she said wistfully.

Lionel Eden eyed her with misgivings for a moment, and then he came to a sudden decision. "I see no reason why you should not," he said. "It is only a short distance, and if we get an early start, we should be able to return to town by late afternoon."

As she smiled at him in delight, sanity returned. "But I do not think your mother will permit such an expedition, even at your age, m'lady," he said, shaking his head. "No, I was not thinking, for it will not do."

Kitty's hands formed fists in her lap, and she made herself take a deep breath. "But if Em'ry came too, how could she object?" she asked. "And I would not hold you up, you know. I ride very well, even my father says so. Oh, do say we may do it, m'lord! It will be an adventure, and I have not had an adventure for months!"

The viscount laughed at her, throwing his head back in that gesture she remembered so well. "I doubt very much that a sedate ride to Maidenhead in company with your brother and me could be classified as an adventure, m'lady," he told her when he could speak again. "At least, for the sake of my reputation, we must hope that will be the case. Now, when shall we go?"

"Oh, let us go tomorrow," Kitty pleaded, not wanting to give him any time to reconsider the plan lest he change his mind. "I am sure Em'ry will be able to join us then, but I will send you word. How early should we be ready to start?"

"Shall we say at nine?" the viscount suggested. "Thank heavens you are not a woman grown, Miss Kittycat," he added. "If you were, you would be horrified to be about at that hour, and it would take you until noon to be ready."

Kitty swallowed. *You will never know how I wish I were,* she said silently. *And I could be ready at six, if that were the hour you set, dear Lion.*

The viscount rose and stretched. "I must be on my way, m'lady," he said. Kitty rose as well. She wished he might remain for hours yet, but knowing she was to see him all day tomorrow made it easier for her to let him go.

Her brother came in an hour later, and his face lit up when she told him about the expedition. "But you must help me convince Mama that it is all right for me to join you, Em'ry," Kitty said, her big eyes never leaving his face.

Her brother shrugged. "I do not see why you are so intent on it, Kitty, but since you are, I will do my best."

Lady Deane was most reluctant when the scheme was explained to her at tea, saying she could not like her daughter's riding about the countryside for the whole day.

"Oh, please, say I may go, Mama!" Kitty begged. "I have not been out of town for such a long time, and I am bored. And this is the first time I will have any fun since we arrived in London!"

Lady Deane eyed her daughter over her teacup. She saw the fervent pleading in her eyes, the way she was sitting on the very edge of her chair, her hands clasped tightly in her lap. Still she was tempted to deny the treat when she remembered the Dowager Duchess of Wynne's startling revelations. It was only that she placed so little credence in them even now, and her very real feeling of guilt that she had neglected Kitty in her preoccupation with her older daughter's future, that made her agree at last.

Kitty hugged her before she ran from the room to write a note to Lion, then hurry up to her room to inspect her best habit. She wished it were not so girlish, but at least it was new, and a becoming shade of dark green, and she had a saucy little hat to wear with it.

The trio set out only a few minutes after nine the following morning. Kitty had been awake at dawn, afraid the day would threaten rain and cause a cancellation. But another one of her prayers had been answered, for it appeared it was going to be warm and sunny.

They arrived at Benning at eleven. The rosy-bricked manor house was as attractive as the viscount had claimed, although somewhat overpowered by unpruned ivy vines. Inside, it was evident that no one had used it for years. Kitty ignored the dust, the peculiar shapes of the furniture shrouded under Holland covers, and the unused smell. She could see the viscount's elderly butler was in a state of shock, as he hurried away to tell his wife a repast would be required in an hour or so. Lion, Emery, and Kitty decided to fill the time by riding over the land, since none of them had much interest in inspecting the house.

Only a few fields had been planted, the rest lying fallow and neglected. Several of the tenant farmers' cottages were vacant as well. The viscount's face grew grimmer as he saw the negligence of what could be such a prosperous property. At the agent's house, he excused himself and went in to see the man alone. Kitty and her brother dismounted to inspect a wide stream nearby.

"Benning is a pretty place, isn't it, Em'ry?" Kitty asked, admiring the fields covered with wildflowers.

"It would be prettier if it were well cared for, and planted in crops," her brother said. "Lord, what was Lion thinking of to let it get in such a state?"

"He has been away," Kitty said hotly in his defense. "How could he see to its care, on the other side of the Atlantic?"

Emery Cahill pulled one of her curls. "No need to ruffle up, puss," he said easily. "But even I, as little as I know of such things, would have thought he might have had his man of business ride out now and again to inspect the place." He shrugged. "It reminds me that I had better take more of an interest in Deane. I've left it all to Pa for too long."

"He would be pleased, I'm sure," Kitty told him as she bent to pick a daisy. Idly, she stripped the petals, whispering to herself, "He loves me, he loves me not . . ."

The daisy told her he loved her not, but she was not disheartened. Not now he doesn't, she admitted, but he will!

The viscount's usually good-natured face was black

when he rejoined them. Neither Cahill would have questioned him, but he spoke immediately, telling them that he had ordered the agent off his land by nightfall. "I shall see about replacing him with someone more dependable at once," he said, his voice grim.

"I am so glad to hear you say so, m'lord," Kitty said, looking beyond her brother who was riding between them. "But after the Season is over, it might be wise for you yourself to come here and oversee its restoration. Benning could be profitable with the proper care. And it is so close to town, you could ride out often if the house was made ready for you. And I see no reason why Benning could not be used to produce those things that are so expensive in town—fresh eggs, country hams, flour and wheat. Why, if you repaired the hothouse, you might even supply early green vegetables and flowers!"

She saw Emery was staring at her, and she flushed as she subsided. But Lionel Eden was smiling at her as he said, "Well thought on, m'lady, and my intention, too."

As the three cantered up the drive to the manor a few minutes later, they saw a light racing curricle pulled up before the door. Kitty frowned. Who could it be? She wanted no one else to interfere with the time she spent alone with the viscount. Why, she had already resented Emery's presence a little today, and now there were other visitors. It was too bad!

The trio halted their mounts near the carriage, and Kitty's eyes widened as she saw the older man who had become such a special friend of the viscount's helping a very luscious blond out of the carriage. She was dressed in a revealing gown of scarlet that was much too ornate for the countryside. Kitty saw Lion's face brighten for a moment before he turned to see her watching him. At once, a frown replaced his grin, and she wondered why. As he dismounted and went to greet his unexpected guests, Kitty heard Emery mutter, "Well, here's a to-do! Mama will not like to have you in such company, puss. It's not at all the thing!''

"Surely we don't have to tell her, do we?" Kitty asked as she slid down into his arms. "Is that Lion's opera dancer, Em'ry?"

Her brother looked astounded. "What do you mean? And what do you know about opera dancers? You hold your tongue, Kitty, or I'll take you home at once!"

Kitty promised to be good as they walked to where the others were standing. She saw Sir Nigel St. Edmunds had raised his quizzing glass to inspect her again, and that the voluptuous blond who was clinging so closely to the viscount's arm was pouting.

"I still do not understand why you came out here, Nigel," Lionel Eden was saying as they approached. His face was as dark as any thunderhead.

"But, my dear boy, when I drove around to your rooms this morning, your excellent man told me of your visit to the family acres. Learning it was located such a short distance from town, and the day was so pleasant, I decided on the spur of the moment to join you. And bring Dorcas with me. So dreary, these affairs of business, are they not? It was the least we could do to support you, our friend, on the occasion. But now it appears you are not glad to see us. How am I to take that, I wonder?"

The viscount betrayed his youth by flushing. Kitty saw he was disconcerted by the mere suggestion that he was being rude.

"Of course I am glad to see you, Nigel, and—and Dorcas, too. But I do not know if the two elderly servants who have been holding household here will be prepared for a further invasion of guests," he said.

"But if that is all, you must not worry, dear boy," Sir Nigel assured him. He beckoned to his groom, who reached into the carriage to remove a large, covered basket. "You see *we* are well prepared, for we have brought a picnic with us. One never knows what one will require in rural locations, after all. And your, er, companions are most welcome to join us in our repast, are they not, my dear?''

Miss Dorcas nodded, still inspecting Kitty's slender form and bright red hair. ''If Lion wanth'em, I'm sure ith no never mind to me,'' she said in a breathless little girl's voice. Kitty had to hide a grin. She had never met a demimonde, but somehow she had thought they would have sultry voices, full of second meanings. She had never imagined one of them would lisp, or have such a common accent. But of course, she reminded herself, Lion does not care how she *talks*!

''Are we to be kept standing about indefinitely, Lion?'' Sir Nigel asked somewhat plaintively. ''And you have not presented us to your young friends.''

The viscount started, and recalled to his manners, introduced the Cahills to his newest guests. His voice sounded constricted as he did so, and Kitty was as formal as she could be in her greeting. She did not curtsy. Her brother's voice was also stiff and cold, and he stayed very close to her side, which seemed to amuse Sir Nigel greatly.

The meager repast that the housekeeper had produced was more than augmented by the contents of the picnic basket, and although it could not be said that it was a merry party that sat down around the newly dusted dining table, at least it was one that would not go hungry. There were meat pastries, breast of squab, and an assortment of cheeses, as well as crusty rolls, luscious grapes, frosted cakes and an excellent wine. Miss Dorcas Watts ignored everyone but the viscount, much to that gentleman's embarrassment. It was left to Sir Nigel and Emery Cahill to conduct a conversation as best they could, for Kitty was silenced by the obvious full-blown charms of Lion's opera dancer, and her caressing behavior.

When the baronet would have poured her some wine, her brother turned her glass over. "My sister does not drink spirits, sir," he said.

Sir Nigel's brows rose. "But, of course, what was I thinking of?" he murmured, filling his own glass instead. "She is only a child as yet. Perhaps you should send for a pitcher of milk, Lion?"

Kitty gripped her hands together under the cover of the table as he went on to make much of her innocence and tender years. "In fact, dear boy, I am surprised her mother let her come here, and with *you*, of all people," he concluded.

Before the viscount could reply, Kitty said, "But we are kin, sir. And of course, my mother did not know that you would be here. Or, er—Miss Watts, was it?— either," she added, nodding to the opera dancer.

That lady trilled a spiteful little laugh that Kitty thought as grating as a fingernail on a slate. "Coo 'er!" she said. " 'ow orful! Shall we go away, Lion?"

She leaned toward him and opened her mouth for one of the grapes he was holding. Kitty was glad when the viscount handed her a bunch of her own. She could not have borne watching him feed the woman, as common and obvious as she was.

After luncheon, the baronet insisted on inspecting the manor and the gardens. "Do you plan to put the place in order, Lion?" Sir Nigel asked after a while in his light, high voice.

At the viscount's assent, he said smoothly, "Capital! It will make an excellent *pied à terre* for you, my friend. And since it is so close to town, you can have the most delightful and, er, unusual parties here. I shall be pleased to help you plan them."

Kitty wondered why Lion's face reddened under his tanned skin, and why her brother stiffened even more. What was there about Sir Nigel's offer to cause such a reaction? And what kind of parties was he referring to? She decided she would have to ask Emery later, before she realized she could not do that, for he would not tell her a single thing. She sighed, for she would have loved to have heard about an orgy.

It seemed only a short time later before the viscount insisted they all must return to town. Kitty was disappointed, for she had hoped to spend the afternoon at Benning, and perhaps have a chance to talk to Lion alone.

As Dorcas Watts clung to the viscount's arm, and whispered in his ear so he was forced to draw her a little apart, Emery went to fetch the horses. He could hardly wait to get his little sister away away from here, and he prayed she would have enough sense to hold her tongue when they were back in town. If his mama ever found out, he would never hear the end of it!

Left alone with Sir Nigel, Kitty decided she would not speak to the man. He eyed her in the lengthening silence, his lip curling in amusement, and she felt a stab of anger. Why was it he could make her feel so gauche, so young and inconsequential?

"I am afraid our driving out was not such a good idea after all," he drawled now. "Do forgive me, m'lady, but you see, I had no idea that such a proper, *pure* young lady was to be in the party. You are hardly Lion's general preference in female companionship."

His voice seemed to mock her innocence, and Kitty nodded slightly. Sir Nigel made her more than uneasy. She felt all ashiver just standing beside him. Somehow, in some way, she knew she had to get the viscount away from this evil man before it was too late. She did not know why she felt this so strongly, she only knew that it was so. Lionel Eden was in grave danger, and like a cat protecting her lone kitten, Lady Catherine was prepared to fight for him with all the weapons at her disposal.

When she made no reply, Sir Nigel stared at her. He saw the disdain and revulsion in her speaking green eyes. He also saw her defiance, and his own dark brown eyes narrowed.

"But I see that it is to be war between us, m'lady," he murmured, as his lips tightened. "Am I correct?"

Kitty widened her eyes, as if in confusion.

"And somehow I have the feeling that you will be a worthy adversary, in spite of your tender years. You look just like a furious kitten," the baronet told her. "I shall be on my mettle, you may be sure."

"As I shall, sir," Kitty told him, stung into replying at last. "Remember that kittens have claws, and sharp teeth as well."

"How dauntless of you, my dear child," he said, looking a little amused now. "But claws and teeth notwithstanding, I do not think your weapons adequate to the task. Not yet, at any rate."

His eyes swept her figure in a slow, insolent inspection, and she turned away to hide a gasp. "For I must tell you that although there are many men who delight in virginal children, and the younger the better, Lionel Eden is not one of them. It is too bad . . . for you."

Lady Catherine wondered what was keeping her brother. She saw the viscount handing the opera dancer into the carriage, and beckoning to Sir Nigel then, and she drew a deep breath of relief.

After the two men had said good-bye and the carriage began to move away, Kitty moved back to Lion's side. She saw Emery coming up from the stables, leading a horse. He was followed by an old groom with the other two.

"I must humbly beg your pardon, Lady Catherine," the viscount said hastily, as if he wanted to speak to her alone. "I would never have subjected you to such company, never! And if your mother finds out you were even introduced to them, she will have my head for it! But you must believe that I had no idea that they would join us!"

Kitty pressed his arm. "Of course I believe you," she said as she smiled up at him, feeling heady at being so close to him. "But I was surprised that they are friends of yours, m'lord," she added. "Oh, not so much at Miss Watts, of course. I quite understand her position in your life."

She saw the color burning on his cheekbones, and before he could reply, she went on, "She is pretty, but she has such a funny voice! And I was so afraid she was going to fall out of her gown. Do all opera dancers dress that way, even in the daytime? I am sure they must be more beautiful under the lights on stage, and at a distance."

Seeing the viscount was occupied loosening a suddenly too tight cravat, she continued, "But I do wonder at your friendship with Sir Nigel. He is not a nice man at all, and you are. And even though I did not understand some of the things he was saying to me just now, I knew he should not be saying them."

Lionel Eden grasped her arm. "And just what did he say to you, Kitty?" he asked through gritted teeth.

Kitty made herself shrug. "Oh, something about the fact that some men preferred children, although you were not one of them. But whatever could he have meant, m'lord? When I *was* a child, you were always kind to me. But Sir Nigel looked at me in such a way! He—he made me uneasy, and I don't know why."

"He shall not speak to you that way again, my word on it," the viscount told her, his voice grim.

Emery arrived just then, and there was no more time for any private conversation. Kitty let her brother toss her into the saddle with a little lift to her heart. She had made a beginning. True, it was not much of one, but it was a start, and she could see she had given Lionel Eden a great deal to think about.

On the ride back to London, when they stopped at a small inn to rest the horses and take some refreshment, Kitty was quick to turn the conversation to Benning and its possibilities. She was glad to see the viscount's face light up as they talked about it, and he accepted Emery's offer of assistance in setting it to rights with a clap on his old friend's shoulder. Perhaps, Kitty thought as they went out to the horses again, if Lion were to throw himself into Benning's restoration, he might forget the dangerous Sir Nigel. She did not deceive herself in thinking he might forget Miss Dorcas Watts, however.

Lady Catherine was quick to call on the dowager duchess the following morning and tell her everything that had transpired. Her grace frowned when she learned of the unexpected additional guests, and Kitty's fears that the viscount's new friend was leading him into danger.

"I do not know what to do about it, ma'am, and I am so worried," she said, her green eyes clouded. The dowager's lips tightened.

"I rather think I shall have to take a direct hand in this, my dear," the dowager said firmly. As she got up to pace the room in thought, Kitty felt a wave of gratitude for her very welcome assistance.

At last the old lady came back to her seat, a grim little smile on her wrinkled face. "This situation is beyond your scope, dauntless though you may be, my Lady Lochinvar. But do not worry! I am sure to find the perfect solution. But there are a great many preparations to be made before I act. You must be patient, and do nothing yourself, no matter what opportunities present themselves."

Kitty promised she would not, although she did not expect that any would. Lady Deane was very careful to keep men of Sir Nigel's stamp far away from her daughters. And though she longed to warn the viscount away again, Kitty felt that to do so would be most unwise, for it might arouse his suspicions.

Lionel Eden was very busy in the days that followed, and he had little time for Sir Nigel. He told himself it was just as well, for Kitty's artless remarks about his conversation had made him think about the direction he was taking, to have such a man as a friend. True, he was amusing and witty and sophisticated, but there had been times in the past when the viscount had felt uneasy at his lack of morality, and a barely hidden streak of viciousness. But now, being involved in meetings with his man of business, and interviewing for a new agent and additional servants, as well as making flying trips to Benning to oversee the outfitting and cleaning of the manor, enabled him to avoid his inappropriate friend.

The viscount had dismissed the two elderly retainers with a good pension and replaced them with a middle-aged couple chosen for their ability to return the manor house to its former elegance and grace. Lionel Eden was assisted in all his endeavors by Emery Cahill and some other relatives the dowager duchess had had a quiet word with, and slowly but surely, Benning began to look like the gentleman's estate it was.

Her grace also had a great many discussions with a private inquiry agent who called in Berkeley Square on a regular basis.

Two weeks later, Sir Nigel St. Edmunds left the country very late one night, and in such a furtive, hurried manner that his departure was the subject of much speculation among the *ton*. Why he had gone, or where, remained a mystery, however. Lady Catherine Cahill had no idea how the dowager had accomplished this timely and welcome exodus, although she did not doubt for a moment that it was she who had master-minded it.

But when she questioned the lady, her grace refused to discuss it, saying that there were some things that were not suitable for a fifteen-year-old miss to hear, no, not even one as mature as her dear Kitty. The only thing she would say, with that grim little smile on her face, was that she had had no idea she would have such a plethora of wrongdoings from which to choose.

Eight

LADY CATHERINE had hoped she might have a chance to see Benning again before the family left town, but the Season was over before the viscount was ready to show off his property, even to the family. At dinner one evening, shortly before they all left London, he told the Cahills about his accomplishments so far, however. Kitty tried not to be too obvious about it as she stared at his handsome, animated face. She knew he had promised to come to Devon for Lady Millicent's wedding in early September, but there were a great many weeks until then, and she knew how much she would miss him. She felt she was missing him already.

He kissed her cheek in parting, and hugged her, those dark blue eyes twinkling at her in quite his old way. It was all she could do not to throw her arms around him right there in the drawing room. Only her parents' watchful eyes, and the presence of Millie and Emery, deterred her.

The West Country seemed very quiet after all the activity and noise of town. Lady Catherine tried to interest herself in her sister's bridal clothes, and all the happy couple's plans, but her thoughts often went to Benning and Lionel Eden. She wondered how he was, and what he was doing, and she was delighted when her brother returned from a month-long visit there, for now he could tell her all about her love.

Lady Millicent planned a quiet country wedding, for

one of Lord Fitton's great aunts had passed away six
months previously and, under the circumstances, a gala
affair was not considered appropriate. Kitty was sure
Millie must be disappointed, for she knew she had
dreamed of a large, formal wedding in one of London's
great cathedrals. Now, however, she would be married
in the village church, with only her sister in attendance.
Kitty was glad to see that, even so, Millie appeared very
happy.

When she had her gown fitted, Kitty noticed she had
acquired a bit more shape, and that she had grown taller
as well. It will not be long now, she told herself as she
stood patiently for the dressmaker to adjust the hem. In
only another year or so, surely Lion would come to see
she was the girl he had been waiting for all his life.

The September day of Lady Millicent's wedding was
clear and sunny. The bride was breathtaking, and much
exclaimed over, and many of the guests remarked about
her younger sister as well. In a gown of palest primrose,
with a wreath of fresh flowers on her glowing curls,
Lady Catherine was a slim and graceful figure.

At the large party at Deane that followed the
ceremony, Kitty was delighted to see how many gentlemen begged her for a dance, and how the Dowager
Duchess of Wynne beamed at her from her place of
honor at the top of the room. Even Garth Allendon
asked for a dance, and Kitty wondered at his intent look
and the way he squeezed her hand when that dance was
over, before he let her go.

But of course, even though she tried not to show her
interest in one tall, handsome gentleman, Kitty had eyes
only for Viscount Benning. She wondered if Lion would
remember the evening in the upper hall of Wynne, how
he had promised to ask her to dance when she was all
grown up. To her disappointment, he did not, for he
was deep in a discussion with Lord Deane and other
estate owners. For the first time, Kitty resented
Benning, and the hold it had on the viscount.

She went to sit beside the dowager for a while, to catch up on all the news of town. Her grace told her what she wished most to hear—that Lionel Eden had made no plans to return to Jamaica on a permanent basis.

"He has written to his aunt and uncle to tell them he will spend the winter months with them," the dowager said. "But I imagine he is only going to apprise them of his changed plans, and all he hopes to do with Benning. I am certain we will have him with us in the spring, Kitty."

"And I will be sixteen, then, ma'am," Kitty whispered, her eyes sparkling.

"It's early days yet, missy!" the dowager scolded her. "You will just be turned sixteen! Don't be impatient, Kitty. There's time yet, much time."

"But a year takes so long, ma'am," Kitty wailed softly.

The dowager patted her hand. "Yes, to the young a year seems like forever, I know. I do assure you that to someone my age, the days just fly by. Why, it seems only yesterday that I was a girl your age, and look at me now!"

Kitty smiled, but she was not required to answer this amazing remark, for Garth Allendon was bowing before them, and begging that she honor him with the country dance that was about to begin. Kitty sighed to herself as she agreed. The horrid Garth had grown into a good-looking young man, but she still could not like him. Every time she looked at him, she seemed to hear him calling her Tibby, or feel him pulling her braids until she cried with pain.

Lionel Eden never did ask her to dance, and she was so disappointed, she wanted to weep. He had danced with the bride and several other ladies, but not once had he come near her, or even smiled at her. The only one he favored was Millie's old friend, Regina Holden.

He took the lady in to dinner, and spent the rest of the

evening with her. Kitty eyed the pair with misgiving.
She thought it was most unfortunate that Miss Holden
was still unwed, and so very pretty to boot. She had
large dark eyes and clouds of curly hair to match, and a
wild rose complexion. But what was worse, she was the
only child of wealthy parents.

Kitty had always thought her a silly thing, and she
wondered at the viscount's choice. But it was not until
the bridal couple had driven away and he still continued
attentive, that she decided to do something about it.

Following Miss Holden to the ladies withdrawing
room, where she had gone so a maid might repair a
ripped flounce on her gown, Kitty settled down and proceeded to tell her all about Jamaica. Miss Holden was
fascinated, as were the maids, when Kitty told them
about the dangerous former slaves who lived in the
mountains and might be planning an uprising even now;
the giant iguanas and snakes; the poisonous plants.
Warming to her theme, she mentioned the violent hurricanes that destroyed everything in their path, the endless, incessant rainy season. She even invented a large
purple spider with three-inch-long legs whose bite was
known to cause madness. Both the maids' and Miss
Regina Holden's eyes were wide with horror as she
finished, and when they left the room together, Kitty
was delighted to see Miss Holden hurrying to her
mother's side and ignoring the handsome, waiting
viscount completely.

"Now, what have you been up to, Kitty?" her mother
asked, eyeing her daughter's satisfied little smile with
misgivings.

"Why, nothing, Mama," Kitty said. "I have only
been keeping Miss Holden amused by telling her a story
while her gown was being repaired."

Rose Cahill shook her head. From the look on Regina
Holden's face, it must have been quite a story!

But the marchioness was perturbed for quite another

reason. She had been watching Kitty, and today she had come to see that what the dowager had told her this past Season was all too true. For even though Kitty was careful not to stare, her mother had seen her love for Lionel Eden shining in her eyes whenever she thought she was unobserved. She wondered at it, and at her daughter's perseverance as well. And she felt a qualm that this faithful devotion might never be rewarded, no matter what Kitty did. After all, she had seen no sign that the girl's affections were returned. The viscount treated her like the young distant relation she was, and that was all. And it was entirely possible that he would fall in love and marry someone else long before Kitty was old enough to be considered. Why, she had been much struck by the attention he had paid Regina Holden this very evening. Suddenly, Rose Cahill's lips curved in a broad smile as she remembered Kitty's "story." Trust Kitty! She was as clever as she could stare, and her mother thought she just might win through because of it.

And she, herself, admitted she liked the young viscount. She knew her husband would have no objection to him as a future husband for his daughter. It was true, he was not a wealthy man, but that was of small importance to a young lady with Kitty's generous portion. And there was the troublesome possibility that he might have to spend his life in the Indies, but she knew if Kitty wanted him, Reginald would agree to it. Kitty had always had a special place in her father's heart. Reminding herself that her daughter was only fifteen, and there were at least two years before such things became a real concern, she put the problem from her mind as she went to see to her guests' comfort.

The following afternoon, as Lionel Eden was returning to the house from the stables, he heard Miss Holden's voice coming from the direction of the garden.

He would have called out and joined her, except her words suddenly made him pause, a frown on his handsome face.

"Ever since you told me about those purple spiders in Jamaica, Kitty, I cannot be easy out of doors!" Miss Holden was saying. "Brr!"

"But none of them have been brought to this country, my dear Miss Holden," Kitty Cahill's clear young voice assured her earnestly. "However, I am glad we are in England, too. Especially when I think about voodoo."

"Voodoo?" Miss Holden asked, sounding very frightened.

The viscount edged closer, a small grin replacing the frown on his face as he prepared to eavesdrop shamelessly.

"Oh, my, yes," Lady Catherine was saying now. "For you must know there are many practitioners of the black arts on Jamaica. And if someone doesn't like you, they can have a doll made in your image, and a spell cast. Then pins are stuck in the doll until you sicken and die."

"Sicken?" Miss Holden echoed, aghast. "Die?"

"I understand people are very glad to die when the time comes, for they have so much constant pain from the spell," her relentless instructress said.

Viscount Benning had to put his fist over his mouth to stifle his laughter.

"You appear to know a great deal about the West Indies, Kitty," Miss Holden said in a wondering voice. "But how can that be? You have never been there, have you?"

"No, but I became interested when the viscount told me about the island several years ago, and I have read extensively since," Lady Catherine told her. "It is a fascinating place, but I do not think I would care to live there, would you?"

"Oh, no, never!" Miss Holden breathed. "I would never consider it."

There was silence for a moment, and then Lady Catherine said in a pensive way, "Isn't it a shame that Viscount Benning must do so? And for the rest of his life as well?"

"Very sad," Miss Holden agreed. "And yet, perhaps . . . ?" She sighed a little, as if in regret.

A moment or two later, Lady Catherine changed the subject, complimenting her companion on her figured silk gown with its smart braid trimming and matching sarcenet shawl.

"Yes, it is sure to be all the crack," Miss Holden told her, sounding animated and happy for the first time. "It is a new style that other ladies will only be able to copy next Season. How I do adore being first with the latest fashion!"

"You are wise to remain in England, indeed, then," Lady Catherine pointed out. "According to the viscount, ships seldom bother to carry the latest *haut couture* from England, and those few ladies on Jamaica are forced to make do with last year's gowns, or even those of the year before. Of course, there is little socializing, and no balls, so I suppose they do not mind."

"Never say so!" Miss Holden exclaimed, sounding even more horrified now than she had at the thought of having pins stuck into a doll that looked just like her, and dying a lingering, terrible death.

The viscount would have gone away then before he disgraced himself, although he fully intended to take Lady Catherine to task in the very near future, when he heard Miss Holden exclaim, "Oh, there is Lord Fitton's nice older brother, strolling toward the river. Do excuse me, dear Kitty! There is something of particular importance I wish to discuss with him. . . ."

Lionel Eden waited until he was sure the lady was some distance away, and then he strolled around the hedge where he had been hiding. Lady Catherine was seated in the gazebo, her hands folded serenely in her lap as she stared after the lady who had just deserted her. All he could see of her was her patrician profile.

He edged closer, and then he said in his normal voice, "Purple spiders, puss? And voodoo? Now wherever did you hear such things, I wonder? I know it was not from me!"

Lady Catherine jumped, her hands to her heart. As the viscount came up the steps, she saw the purpose in his eyes, and she steeled herself. Why, oh why, had he overheard her? she wondered.

"Yes, the voodoo especially was a whisker, of course," she said as calmly as she could as he settled down in Miss Holden's recently vacated chair. "I know it is practiced on Haiti, not Jamacia, so you will please not take me to task for inaccuracy, m'lord."

She leaned back in her chair then, and a sunbeam caught in her curls, turning them to fire. The viscount did not appear to be at all enchanted by the sight.

"But why did you tell Miss Holden those things?" he persisted. "And do, please, enlighten me about the purple spiders. I have never seen one."

Kitty peeked at him. She did not think he looked angry, in fact for one brief second she had been sure he was trying hard not to laugh. "She was so very interested in Jamaica, and she asked so many questions," Kitty explained. "But—but perhaps I did get a little in alt in describing the island. I do so love to tell a good story!"

"Were you by any chance trying to put paid to any chance I might have with the lady, Miss Kittycat?" he asked sternly.

Kitty opened her green eyes wide. "*Are* you interested in her, m'lord? Oh, dear, then I am afraid I have done a very bad thing indeed."

"I am not in the least interested in her, I was merely flirting," the viscount found himself retorting. He shook his head. "Not that it would do me any good now if I were mad with love for her. For if the purple spiders did not frighten her off, certainly your description of island fashions has ruined any chance I might have had with her. How could Miss Holden possibly survive in a place where she had to wear last year's gown?''

Kitty put her head back and laughed out loud, for she could contain herself no longer. To her delight, it was only a moment before Lionel Eden joined in. ''How ridiculous she is!'' she gasped when she could speak again.

As she took out her handkerchief to wipe her streaming eyes, the viscount said, ''True. But now you will tell me the real reason you did it, puss.''

Lady Catherine began to think, somewhat frantically. She remembered the dowager's warning that girls who made a dead set at a man were quickly abandoned, and she searched her mind for something other than her love for him that he might find plausible.

At last she said slowly, ''I did it to tease her, because she is so gullible.'' She sighed, and then she made herself look into Lionel Eden's dark blue eyes. ''It is very hard to be good when someone believes the most outrageous things you say. I—I am very sorry, m'lord.''

She stared down at her hands then, and held her breath, and she was relieved to hear his little chuckle as he sat back and crossed his breeched legs.

''From what I heard, you were easy to believe,'' he said. ''You spoke of the island as if you had lived there for years. Was it true what you told Miss Holden? That you read a great deal about it after I described it to you at Wynne three years ago?''

Kitty made herself smile at him. He had sounded somewhat wary, and she knew she had to disarm him if she could. ''Yes, I did. You tell a very good story, too, m'lord, and you made me want to know more about it.'' She thought he looked a little puzzled still, and she was quick to add, ''Not that I am blue, you understand! It was just that my governess insisted I study some geography, so I chose the West Indies.''

The viscount smiled now, and she was emboldened to say, "I shall make a complete confession, sir. Besides the strange spiders and black magic, I also told her all about the Maroons whom I claimed were planning a massive uprising, iguanas as big as a man, and plants that poisoned you if you only looked at them."

As the viscount began to chuckle again, she added, "I believe I also mentioned the ferocious hurricanes, and the incessant, dreary rainy season."

The viscount was laughing now, and she grinned at him. "Oh, Kittycat, was there ever such a girl as you?" he asked. "I think you are part witch!"

She shook her head, but when she saw he was about to rise, she was quick to ask him about Benning, and his plans for the winter. The viscount settled back in his chair again.

"I plan to leave England in late October, not wanting to sail through any of your ferocious hurricanes, puss," he told her. "By then, there will be little I can accomplish at Benning until next spring. And, you see, I feel I have to go back. I have to tell my aunt and uncle, face to face, why I cannot stay in Jamaica." His face grew grim. "I hate to think of their disappointment, but I have come to see that that life is not for me. There are more important things than assured wealth."

"I am sure they will understand, Lion," Kitty told him, leaning forward in her eagerness. "They chose their own way; now they must let you choose yours."

The two sat in companionable silence for a moment before Kitty said, "You are sure you will be in London next spring?"

"In England, yes, always barring some unforseen incident. And since I will be at Benning, I do believe I might ride up to town every now and again," he said. "But isn't it amazing, Kitty? I never thought of myself as a landowner, in fact, I was sure I hated the life, for just look at my reaction to Jamaica! But when I saw Benning, its weedy fields and rotting manor, I was furious. It is such good property, with such endless potential, that I was ashamed I had let it fall into such neglect.''

He shook his head, and Kitty said, "But of course! That is *your* land, m'lord, *your* manor. Of course you were angry! But I am sure you will do all you can to restore it.''

Lionel Eden rose now and stretched. "I will, indeed," he said, his voice firm.

"I shall look forward to seeing you in town then, next Season, sir,'' Kitty said, getting up to stand beside him.

The viscount cocked a tawny brow at her. "But will you be there?" he asked. "You are only fifteen, much too young for a Season.''

"I will be sixteen then!" Kitty said so hotly he smiled.

"Almost on the shelf," he said solemnly, although his dark blue eyes twinkled at her.

Kitty forgot herself and grasped his arms tightly. "I am *not* a child now, and most certainly, I shall *not* be one then. Besides, I—I will miss you if you do not come," she added, delicate color washing over her face.

"Thank you, m'lady," he said, and there was no mockery in his voice now. "I do believe I will miss you, too. And if there is snow at Wynne this year, will you take out the big sled and have a slide for me? I shall like to think of you doing so, at Christmas, and I shall envy you, situated as I will be in stormy, strife-ridden, poison-infested Jamaica.''

Kitty nodded, for she had a lump in her throat just thinking of the long months they would be apart.

"Probably I shall not see you again before I sail," the viscount was saying now. "That is why I ask the favor at this time.''

Kitty swallowed. "I know. I wish you God speed, Lion, and a safe return," she said.

She looked up at him then, and caught her breath at his nearness. "Will you kiss me good-bye, Lion?" she asked, helpless in her need to be in his arms, feel his lips on hers, just once.

The viscount hesitated. The red-haired girl with the big green eyes who was so close to him seemed different somehow, and he felt uneasy. But then he reminded himself that this was only Miss Kittycat, after all, the distant cousin he had known since she was a baby. He bent his head and touched her lips lightly with his own.

To his surprise, he felt her arms come up around his neck all in a rush, as she pressed close to him. He had the irrelevant thought that it was very strange he had not noticed how tall she had grown until just now. Then he stood perfectly still as her innocent lips clung to his, and he felt her slim, pliant body melt against him in complete surrender. She was right. She was not a child anymore.

Lost in the spell she wove, he could not tell if it was the perfume of the garden flowers or her own sweet, clean scent that seemed to envelop him. And why did he feel the prick of tears behind his eyelids, the rapid beat of his heart? He told himself that it was because to him, at that moment, Kitty was a symbol of all he loved best about England, everything that he was forced to leave, yet one more time. He was sure that was why, for one mad moment, he had longed to put his own arms around her and hold her close—kiss her as deeply as he had ever kissed any lovely woman.

But Kitty Cahill was not as yet a woman, and she did not know what she was doing. It was up to him, in his maturity, to salvage the situation as best he could, no matter how touching the interlude.

He made himself raise his head and put her away from him. He realized all at once that his little Miss Kittycat was forever gone, and he felt a stab of regret that it was so. He swallowed, and swinging her hands a little, he said, "Thank you, dear Kitty. But I shall be back before you know it. Take care of yourself."

"You take care too, Lion," Kitty said over the

breathless exultation she was experiencing. "Especially around those purple spiders," she forced herself to add lightly. "Oh, I do so hope I just imagined them. How awful if they turned out to be real!"

The viscount's expression brightened as she had hoped it would. She had seen his questioning look, the little frown between his brows, after their kiss, and she had known with an instinct as old as Eve's that this was not the time to tell him of her love. For what could be accepted, even smiled at, as childish infatuation when blurted out by a girl only twelve, could not be considered that way when declared by an almost-full-grown young lady. She must wait, be patient still.

As they strolled back to the house side by side, she told herself that at least now she had something wonderful to remember, something that was uniquely him to hold in her heart all the lonely days and nights until he came back to England—and to her—again.

In December, the Cahills went to Wynne for Christmas. There were only four of them now, for Millicent and her new husband were visiting his family for the holidays.

Kitty told herself she must do her best to enjoy all the familiar customs. She intended to keep a diary while she was at Wynne, and beg her brother to send it to Lionel later. That way, he would not miss all the Christmas festivities he loved.

Katherine Elizabeth and her mother had not come this year, and Kitty was disappointed. She had not seen her friend for a long time, and now she would be the eldest of the children present by several years. How silly she would feel at fifteen in that separate dining salon, surrounded by little ones!

To her surprise, her mother told her as soon as they had arrived that the duchess was making an exception this year. Because of the disparity in ages, she would be happy to have Catherine join the grownups.

Kitty was sure the dowager duchess had had a hand in the decision, but she would have been stunned to learn that it was Garth Allendon who had done the most to champion her cause.

She was on her best behavior that evening, for she could tell that several elderly relations did not like this break with tradition at all. After dinner, she spent a long time with her friend the dowager, exchanging news. Agatha Allendon thought Kitty looked different, and much older somehow, and she wondered if anything had happened between the girl and Lionel Eden at Deane this past September. Kitty, however, had no intention of sharing her memories, not even with this good friend, so the dowager never did find out about that one, wonderful embrace.

When the gentlemen joined them after their port, Kitty was surprised to see how attentive Garth Allendon was to her. In fact, throughout their stay at Wynne, he seemed to be constantly underfoot. She accepted his attentions with resignation for the most part, although at times she was glad he was there, for he was the nearest to her in age. He was always ready to talk to her, or go riding, and when there was a dance, he became her most dependable partner. He little knew that Lady Catherine was only thinking of the absent Lionel Eden as she took her place with him in the sets.

When the kissing ball was hung in the main drawing room, Kitty felt uneasy at Garth's eager smile, the little nod he gave her. She avoided the mistletoe diligently, but one evening, responding to her mother's signal, she passed under it without thinking. As the others laughed, Garth caught her from behind and gave her a hug and a hearty kiss. Kitty's face was aflame when she pulled away from him, and, as soon as she could, she excused herself to go to her room. As she scrubbed her face and lips with a soapy washcloth, she shivered with rage. She was Lion's! And now she felt that the lips that had known the viscount's kiss had been defiled.

Lady Catherine was careful to stay close to her mama from that time on, much to that lady's amusement and Garth Allendon's regret. The dowager duchess chuckled to herself. She knew very well why Lady Catherine did not give a snap of her fingers for her first conquest, even if he was a duke's son and an excellent catch!

Throughout her stay at Wynne, Lady Catherine had watched the sky with anxious eyes. It had been a wet autumn with many rainy days, but now that the weather had turned cold, there was not a cloud in the sky. Not once had even a dusting of snow covered the ground, and the day that she would have to leave for Devon was fast approaching. Would she have to go home before she could keep her promise to Lion?

So when she woke up one January morning to discover it had snowed heavily during the night, not even the most enthusiastic of the nursery children was more pleased than Lady Catherine Cahill.

She waited that afternoon until all the children had left the sledding hill, and only then did she go to the stables alone and ask for the big sled. It was almost dusk when she stood at last on the top of the big hill, her thoughts far away. With all her might, she willed Lion to be thinking of her, and Wynne, and England. And then she took her seat on the sled, picked up the steering rope, and pushed off. She closed her eyes as it gathered speed, hoping that in doing so she might conjure up the shadow of his strong arms around her, his legs imprisoning her body; become his willing captive again.

But there was only the cold wind of her passage whistling by her ears, and the squeak of the runners on the dry, crisp snow. She had never felt so bereft, so alone.

At the bottom of the hill when the sled finally glided to a stop, she sat slumped over for a moment in the silence, trying hard not to cry. He was so far away, and she missed him so!

It was a long and lonely climb back up the hill to the

north face of Wynne, and, when she reached it, Kitty
did not turn the sled around and take another run.
Instead, she dragged it back to the stables. She had kept
her promise to Lion, but she would not go sledding ever
again, she told herself. Not until they could go together.

Before she entered the palace, she paused to make her
usual wish on the evening star. Dreaming and far away,
she was startled when Garth Allendon took her arm and
smiled down at her. He seemed very disappointed when
he learned she had returned the sled, and he begged her
to come out with him for at least one more run. Kitty
refused, almost brusquely.

As she ran inside, the disconsolate young peer stared
after her. Unwittingly, Kitty had done precisely what
the dowager had told her to do to catch a suitor. Garth
Allendon nodded his head, his lips tightening. Kitty
Cahill was growing up to be one of the most intriguing,
fascinating females he had ever met in all his nineteen
years. He knew he would never forget the feel of her in
his arms, her lips beneath his that brief second under the
kissing ball, no, not as long as he lived. And although he
knew she was too young to marry, he had decided he
would be happy to wait for her. After all, it would only
be for two years, he told himself as he followed her
inside.

Kitty copied her diary of Christmas in her best handwriting, carefully removing all references to her love for
Lion and her yearning for that day when they would be
together at last. The only time her pen slipped was when
she told him how she had felt at the bottom of the
sledding hill, and even those words only mentioned how
she missed him. She had been quick to add that
everyone else had missed him as well.

Several weeks after Emery had sent the diary off for
her, she was summoned to the morning room by her
mother. A little surprised, for they had just enjoyed
breakfast there minutes before, Kitty rejoined her. As

she curtsied and took the seat her mother indicated, she wondered at the lady's stern, unsmiling expression.

Then she saw that the post had been delivered, and that her mother was holding a sheet of paper before her.

"I have a letter here for you, Kitty," she began, frowning a little as she looked down at it. Kitty clasped her hands together tightly. Oh, pray, let it be from Lion! she implored silently. Her wide green eyes searched her mother's face, but she did not speak.

"It is from Viscount Benning," her mother went on. "Quite correctly, he wrote to me and enclosed it in my letter so I might read it first."

Kitty leaned forward. "You have read my letter, Mama?" she asked, her voice indignant.

Lady Deane frowned, and her daughter subsided, lowering her eyes at the displeasure she saw in her mother's.

"But of course I did," Lady Deane said. "As your mother it was my duty to do so, as Lionel knew very well. But it is not his letter that displeases me, Kitty, no, not at all. There is nothing in it that the whole world might not see. I did not expect anything else from the young man, of course. He is of good character, and he does just as he ought. No, what displeases me, nay, angers me, is to discover that you have been writing to him, and without my express permission. And now, daughter, you will tell me why you did such an outrageous thing?"

Kitty stared at her mother helplessly. There was no sound in the cheerful room except for the hissing of one of the spirit lamps on the sideboard, and outside the closed door, the measured footsteps of the butler as he went toward the front hall.

"I did it because he said he would be so lonesome in Jamaica, and missing Christmas at Wynne," she said at last, trying hard to keep her voice even. "So, while we were there, I kept a diary of everything that happened. Emery mailed it for me when we returned home."

"But why didn't you ask me or your father to mail it, miss?" Lady Deane asked, her voice stern.

"I—I was afraid you would not permit it, Mama," Kitty whispered, hanging her head.

"Look at me, Kitty!" her mother commanded, and she raised her head obediently. Her mother could see the sick misery in her eyes, and in spite of her anger, her heart went out to her daughter.

"You think you are in love with Lionel Eden, don't you, my dear?" she surprised herself by asking.

Kitty's eyes did not leave her face. "I do not *think* I am, I *know* I am, Mama," she whispered. "I have loved him ever since I was twelve."

The marchioness stared at her younger daughter. She saw the determination in her eyes, the steadfastness, and she sighed. This was no Lady Millicent she had here, to be scolded and manipulated for her own good. This was a young woman who knew her own mind. For a fleeting moment, Lady Deane wished she might have borne two Millicents, for she could see nothing but trouble ahead. And then she chastised herself for such an unworthy thought. Kitty was her dear daughter, no matter what the future might bring.

"I see," she said slowly, laying Lionel Eden's letter down beside her plate.

"It is strange," she mused, as if to herself. "The dowager duchess told me the same thing a year ago, but I did not believe her. And even when I saw for myself how you looked at him at Millie's wedding, I still did not believe it to be anything but infatuation, a young girl's artless worship of a handsome older man."

"It is not like that, Mama," her daughter told her.

Lady Deane sighed again. "So you say. But Kitty, you are only fifteen, and Lionel Eden is almost twenty-four. You must realize that there is every chance that he will fall in love with another before you are of an age for marriage. And even if he does not, he may never return your affection."

She saw Kitty was looking mulish, her lower lip pushed out in the familiar pout of her childhood. "My dear girl," she said tenderly, "I would not have you hurt. You cannot *make* someone love you, Kitty. No, not even you can do that. And I would not have you waste your life in sad regret."

Lady Catherine raised her chin. "But that is a chance I must take—don't you see, Mama?—because I know I can never love another."

Her mother rose then, and came to put her arms around her and hug her close. "Oh, Kitty, how very young you are, to be sure!" she said. "You must believe me when I tell you that the day will most certainly come when you will find yourself in love with another man!" She stood up then, and smiling, she wiggled her finger under Kitty's nose. "But I promise I will not remind you of your impassioned words then, my dear!"

Kitty took a deep breath. "You don't understand, Mama!" she cried, using the words that had been said by so many daughters before her, that would be said by so many others in the future as well.

Perhaps Lady Deane remembered saying them to her own mother, for she did not reprimand Lady Catherine for insolence. Instead, she picked up the viscount's letter and handed it to her. "Here, you may read it now, Kitty," she said.

As Lady Catherine took the page with barely suppressed eagerness, she added, "But this must be the end of any communication between you and Viscount Benning. For even though you are distant relatives, you are much too old for such carrying on."

Kitty was staring down at her name, written in Lion's distinctive handwriting, and she did not appear to hear. Lady Deane clapped her hands.

"Attend me well, miss!" she said sharply, and she waited until Kitty raised her eyes to her face. "I said you may not write to him again, nor shall I permit you to receive any letters from him. Is that understood?"

She saw Kitty was looking rebellious, and she added, "Since you seem so eager to throw your cap over the windmill where the young man is concerned, it is clearly my duty to have a care for your reputation. Know that I shall expect your obedience in this matter."

Kitty took a steadying breath and rose. "Of course, Mama," she said quietly, surprising Lady Deane considerably. "It will be as you say. But you will not forbid Lion to visit when he comes back to England this spring, will you?"

"Of course not," Lady Deane said. "He is our dear relative, and he is always welcome. At least he will be if you behave yourself, miss!"

Kitty curtsied, and waited until her mother waved her hand in dismissal. Only then did she move slowly to the door, and close it softly behind her. Rose Cahill's eyes were bleak as she listened to the sound of her running feet hurrying up the stairs to the privacy of her own room, no doubt with the viscount's letter crushed to her breast. Poor Kitty, her mother thought as she poured herself another cup of tea. But then, she has always been like this—passionate, full of conviction, and sure of herself—so why am I surprised? Pray she will survive this storm without being broken by it, she thought.

Upstairs, behind her closed door, Kitty devoured the single sheet Lion had written, and then she read it over slowly, savoring every word. He thanked her first for her account of Christmas at Wynne, telling her how much it had meant to him to hear everything that had happened. He told her he was well, how he was making plans to return to England in April, and he assured her he was being careful of spiders of any color. He closed his letter by asking her to remember him to everyone in the family, and he signed it, "Yr. Ob't Servant, Lionel Eden."

Kitty put her cheek against his signature and closed her eyes. Her mama was right. It was a letter the entire world might have read, but, even so, it was hers, and hers alone. And it was the first letter she had ever had from him, and if her mama continued relentless, and somehow she was sure that good lady would, perhaps the last. She would keep it forever.

From that day, Lady Catherine began counting the hours until the Season began, and every morning she would lie in bed and wonder if Lion was even then on the high seas, perhaps standing at the rail of his ship, his sun-streaked auburn hair tossed by the wind, and his dark blue eyes eager as he searched the horizon for his first glimpse of home. It was a bitter blow to learn two weeks later that he was not coming at all.

He had written to her brother Emery, of course, so she only heard about it secondhand. It seemed his uncle was ill with a fever, and the viscount did not feel he could leave his aunt at this time. She was distraught and very apprehensive about her husband, and there was the plantation and mill to see to until things returned to normal.

Kitty knew it was evil of her to hate Lion's relatives so, but she could not help resenting the way they clung to him and his young strength. It was not fair! she told herself. Lion has his own life to live, and so do I!

Nine

IT WAS NOT until August, seven long months later, that Lady Catherine learned that Viscount Benning was on his way home at last. The dowager sent her word as soon as she herself heard the news, adding at the end of her letter that she had written to Lady Deane and suggested that Kitty might enjoy visiting her in town during the Little Season in the fall.

When she discussed the possibility with her mother, Kitty thought her most reluctant. Rose Cahill did not feel she could leave Deane at this time, for she had been away for some months, and she knew her husband and her household needed her. And she hesitated at allowing her daughter to visit the Dowager Duchess of Wynne alone. She was aware the viscount was coming home at last, and she was not entirely sure that Kitty would act with becoming deportment in his heady company.

Kitty Cahill knew what was bothering her mother, and one morning as they sat together busy with some sewing, she addressed her concerns directly.

"I know you fear I will not behave myself, Mama, but you are wrong," she said, putting down her sewing to look straight into her mother's eyes. "I will not do anything to disgrace you, I promise. And it would mean so much to me to be there."

"I cannot like it, Kitty," her mother said, a stern look coming over her face. "You will not be seventeen until next spring. Why, you are much too young to be jauntering about this way! I don't know what people would think of me to be allowing it!''

''But no one could take umbrage at my going to stay with the dowager, Mama,'' Kitty pointed out, her tone reasonable. ''Besides, Emery can escort me to town, and I do assure you on my honor, the dowager has given up any jauntering about, at her age.''

Rose Cahill's expression brightened a little at the jest, but it was two more long weeks before her consent could be gained. And even then she might not have agreed, except Kitty went to her father to get his support. That good man was not proof against his favorite child's pleading, and he won his wife over to their side.

Kitty set her maid to packing at once, and wrote a note to the dowager telling her when she would arrive and thanking her for her most welcome invitation.

The night before she was to leave for London, she was so excited she could not sleep. At last she lit her candle again and got up to pace the room. Lion was on his way to England, and soon—soon—she would see him again.

Turning, she caught a glimpse of herself in the mirror and she went up to it to inspect herself carefully.

A tall, slim girl looked back at her as she stared into the glass. In her modest white nightgown and with her tangled red curls hanging down her back, she looked even younger than she was. But as Kitty stared into her own eyes, she saw a woman's heart there, and she knew Lion would see it, too. And as she turned this way and that, smoothing her nightgown tightly against herself, she saw a woman's body; the high rounded breasts and slim waist, the gentle swelling of hips and buttocks, and the long, shapely legs. That she was still sixteen did not matter at all. At last she was a woman grown.

The journey seemed endless to Kitty, even though Emery insisted the coachman set a spanking pace. And it was not until the coach turned into Berkeley Square some three days later that Kitty was able to sigh in relief.

Emery did not stay. An old crony had invited him to share his rooms, so rather than open Deane House or disconcert the dowager, he was off after paying his respects to the old lady and supervising the unloading of his sister's baggage.

The two friends, one so old and one still so untried, sat on together in the drawing room after he left them. Kitty wondered why the dowager seemed so stiff and withdrawn, why her eyes were so sad. Even Miss Jane and Miss Eliza had not come to welcome her as yet. It was most unusual.

And then she had a terrible premonition that it all had to do with the viscount. Perhaps his ship had been lost in a storm! Perhaps he was not coming at all!

"What is the matter, ma'am?" she asked, feeling somewhat breathless. As the dowager considered her seriously, she added, "There is something wrong, isn't there? I can tell by your face! Tell me what it is, please!"

Agatha Allendon sighed. "Come and sit here, my dear," she said, patting the sofa beside her. Numbly, Kitty took the seat she indicated, and the dowager picked up her hand and held it between both of her own. Wildly, Kitty began to pray.

"I have some bad news for you, puss, and I wish with all my heart that I did not," the dowager said. "Lionel Eden arrived in London four days ago, but he did not come alone."

She paused, and Kitty tried to still her fast-beating heart. "Who came with him, ma'am?" she asked in a quiet, even voice.

"A Miss Mary Gardner," the dowager said. "She is his fiancée."

There was silence in the drawing room then, and the dowager peered into Kitty's face, much concerned. The girl sat as still as any statue, as if the words she had just heard had turned her to stone. Only the fast-beating pulse in her throat, and the rise and fall of her breasts under her neat traveling gown, showed that she was not made of marble.

"His fiancée?" Kitty echoed, through stiff lips.

"Yes. He met her in Jamaica when she came to visit her uncle's plantation. While she was there, her mother, who had accompanied her, died. It was then that Lionel thought to bring her home with him, even though their marriage must be postponed for a year of mourning. Her uncle and another relative came with them, as I understand it. They are all to stay with a cousin here in town."

As she finished speaking, Kitty withdrew her hand and rose to her feet. The dowager peered with misgiving at her frozen expression, those eyes that looked as if all the light in them had been extinguished.

"Kitty, my dearest girl!" she cried. "I am so sorry to be the bearer of such bad news. But you always knew there was a chance that Lionel would fall in love before you were old enough to catch his eye. Unfortunately, that has occurred. And not even Lord Lochinvar himself could have won through if his fair Ellen had loved another man. You must be brave and accept it, for there is nothing you or anyone can do to change his mind."

"Have you seen her? And—and him?" Kitty whispered in a dead little voice.

The dowager nodded. "Yes, he came to call and brought her with him so he might present her," she said.

"What is she like?" Kitty asked.

"She is a very nice young woman," the dowager replied slowly, as if she were reluctant to have to admit it. "She is in her twenties, indeed, I believe her to be a year or two older than the viscount. And she is lovely, with dark brown hair and eyes to match. I found her pleasant, although very quiet; a most restful person. Perhaps that is because of her loss, her grief. Lion was most attentive and concerned. And he was quieter, too.

There is no doubt that association with her has tempered his mercurial nature."

"Is the viscount in town now?" Kitty asked next.

"No, he went to Benning almost immediately to oversee the beginning of the harvesting. Miss Gardner, of course, remains here."

The dowager's voice died away as she watched Kitty take a few blind steps. Suddenly, the girl turned back to her old friend, who could not restrain a cry at the tears she saw coursing down her cheeks. Rising, and ignoring the china lovebirds she swept to the carpet with the fringe of her shawl, she hurried forward to fold her close. "My dear, dear girl! You must be very brave now," she murmured.

Lady Catherine slumped in her arms for only a moment. Then she straightened up and gave the dowager a hug before she stepped back, dashing a hand across her cheeks as she did so. She had stopped crying, although traces of her tears were plain to see on her young cheeks.

"Yes, I will be brave," she said. "But right now you must excuse me, dear ma'am. I—I would be alone for a while."

The dowager nodded, although she looked puzzled. It was very unlike Kitty to take this all so meekly, she thought. She had expected her to cry out, rage against fate in her disappointment, for she was still a young girl. Instead, with a maturity she had never imagined her to possess, she had accepted the inevitable quietly.

She continued to watch the girl as she curtsied and left the room, her back straight and her shoulders squared.

When the door closed behind her, the dowager sat down again and shed a few tears herself before she summoned her butler and asked him to bring her a glass of sherry. She felt she needed it.

Agatha Allendon was not surprised when Kitty sent her a message later, begging to be excused from joining her for dinner. Both Miss Jane and Miss Eliza were concerned, and would have gone to her, but the dowager refused to allow it. She knew that Kitty needed some time by herself, before she would be able to face the world.

When the dowager came downstairs at her regular time the next morning, she discovered that her guest had gone out riding very early. When the butler told her of it, he presented a note Kitty had left for her. A little perturbed, she went into the breakfast room and took her seat before she opened it.

Since both her companions had gone out on an errand, there was no one to hear her startled exclamation as she read her message. Kitty had written to say that she intended to ride out to Benning, but the dowager was not to worry about her.

"I have appropriated one of your grooms, dear ma'am," she wrote. "And I will be back before evening. You see, I had to see Lion myself, hear from his own lips that he is engaged and lost to me. And to hear how such an alliance came about. No one knows I am in town except Emery, and he will not come to call today, so no one will know I am gone. Forgive me for leaving without seeing you and asking your permission, but this is something I had to do."

The dowager crumpled the note in her hands. She was not at all surprised, now that she thought it over. This was the Kitty Cahill she had always known, full of fire and passion, sure of her convictions, determined to find her own way. She prayed the viscount would handle her gently, and understand when she told him of her love, as the dowager was sure she would. For even if she refrained from voicing it, her arrival at Benning alone, and the grieving expression in her eyes, would make it very clear.

Kitty Cahill had not been able to sleep for a very long

time the night before. Surprisingly, she had not wept again when she first gained the privacy of her room, for she felt only a frozen numbness, as if all her senses had been drugged. Instead, she had paced back and forth, reviewing everything the dowager had told her. He was lost to her!—gone!—in love with someone else! He had not waited as she had begged him to, he had never even given her the chance to show him how much she cared. Instead, he fallen under another girl's spell. But no, Kitty reminded herself, not a girl, a woman older than he was himself, for so the dowager had told her. A woman full grown and experienced. A quiet, pretty woman who no doubt adored him, and so could not be persuaded by any means to give him up. For that had been Kitty's first plan of action when at last she sank down into a chair to think. She shall not have him! she had told herself fiercely. He is mine, he has always been mine! I will not, *cannot,* let him go! But knowing so well his charm and his handsome good looks, his kindness—all his wonderful qualities—she had known there was no way she could force this Miss Gardner to break their engagement. No way she could prevent their marriage short of murdering her. And for one wild moment, she had even contemplated that. But of course, if Lion loved her, her demise would only bring him pain. And even now, in all her grief, Kitty knew she could never cause him pain.

It was much later, after her maid had been dismissed for the night, still shaking her head over how little Lady Catherine had eaten from her dinner tray, that Kitty's feelings began to change. She was tired now, but she knew she could not sleep. She had heard the other inhabitants of the house making their way to bed sometime earlier, and she had been thankful for the dowager's understanding and sensibility. She could not have borne being fussed over by the three old ladies. Not just yet. Besides, she had to think.

But she was a little amazed when she began to feel angry as well as regretful as she stared down into the dark, silent square beneath her window.

How *could* Lion do this to her? How could he walk away from her after all her years of devotion? How could he treat her love so casually? For he knew of it, he had known of it all this time. Surely he must remember how she had whispered of it on the steps of Wynne that cold January day. Surely he must remember the kiss she had given him less than a year ago at Deane! She thought of it every day, knowing she would never forget it. But he had not remembered or cared. Instead, he had smiled at another woman, talked and laughed with her, taken her in his arms and kissed her. And he had asked her to marry him.

Kitty rose to pace again, her hands clenched into fists at her sides. Well, she would not take this meekly, she vowed. Not for her a mournful acquiescence, a few quiet tears shed at midnight as she contemplated the long, lonely, unfulfilled life that lay ahead. Not Lady Catherine Cahill! She would ride out to Benning and she would see him, and she would tell him how he had ruined her life! Yes, she thought, nodding her head. I shall do exactly that. And I shall do it tomorrow.

Alfred, the groom, accepted her destination with a shrug, when she told him of it the next morning, and of the dowager's permission for the excursion. He would make sure no harm came to the lady in his care, and he knew her for an expert, tireless rider. Even with the necessary stops to rest the horses, he was sure they could return to town in good time.

It was only a little after eleven when they trotted up the drive that led to the manor house. The viscount's butler came out to greet them before Kitty could dismount. He seemed a trifle perturbed when he saw she had no escort other than a groom, but he answered her crisp questions without demur.

Kitty nodded before she sent her attendant to wait for
her at the stables. Then she rode alone to that section of
the estate where the butler had told her the viscount was
working. As she skirted a farm gate and set off across
the fields, she reminded herself that he was lost to her
now, that he had not waited for her after all, that she
would never have him as either her husband or her
lover. And once again, the disappointment and fury she
felt rose up in her breast in a bitter flood she could
almost taste.

She saw him long before he saw her. He was on horseback, supervising the fieldhands busy reaping the tall
corn. Kitty reined in and feasted her eyes on him. He
had removed his jacket and his hat, this warm, almost
sultry September day, and he had opened the neck of his
white shirt and rolled up the sleeves. Kitty could see his
powerful forearms, the deep bronzed skin covered with
curly golden hair. His auburn mane was tousled, and it
glittered with highlights in the bright sunlight. She felt
as if she were staring at a golden god.

Finally, as if aware that he was being observed so
carefully, the viscount turned slightly in the saddle. At
once, his tanned face brightened and his mouth curved
in a welcoming smile. He set his horse to a canter,
waving to her as he came toward her. Kitty sat quietly
and waited. She wanted no meeting before the grinning
harvesters.

"Lady Catherine, well met!" he cried as he reined in
beside her. Still Kitty stared at him, her green eyes
golden with her barely concealed rage. The viscount did
not seem to notice.

"But where's Emery? Is he coming behind? I shall
tease him for being such a slowtop," Lion said as he
dismounted and came to lift her down.

Kitty was quick to unhook her leg from the pommel
and slide down by herself. "He is not coming. I came
out here alone," she said.

Lionel Eden became very still, and he bent his head to stare at her. "You are alone, Kitty? But why is that? You know it is not at all the thing, puss."

"I had to see you," Kitty told him. "I had to ask you myself if what I have heard is true."

Lionel Eden waited, his hands on his hips. In the distance, the sounds of the harvesting could be heard plainly as the corn fell before the farmers' scythes as they advanced in a disciplined line, laughing and chatting with each other. But neither the tall, handsome man, nor the slim red-haired girl facing him was aware of anyone but each other.

"Are you engaged to a Miss Mary Gardner, Lion?" Kitty asked baldly.

She wondered why the viscount seemed to hesitate for a moment, and then she told herself she was imagining things as he nodded, his eyes cool and his expression carefully neutral.

"Yes, I am, m'lady," he said. "Have you come all this way to wish me happy?"

Kitty took an impulsive step toward him, her hand upraised, before she remembered herself. "Wish you happy?" she asked in a hurried, incredulous voice. "I shall *never* wish you happy! How *could* you, Lion? How could you *do* such a thing when I have loved you for such a very long time?"

The viscount's brows rose, and she bit back a sob. No, I must not cry, she told herself. "Oh, are you surprised?" she asked sarcastically. "But that cannot be, for you knew, Lion, you knew. I told you for the first time when I was twelve, and I have not changed since. And that you also knew, from my kiss. Did my love mean so little to you, then?"

He came toward her then. Kitty made herself stand very still as his big hands closed around her upper arms. "Kitty, Kitty," he whispered. "My dear child, you are distraught. And you do not love me at all. I am just another one of the stories you have made up and are loathe to forfeit. No one can love as you claim you do. We are, in spite of our kinship, almost strangers."

"Once before I told you I was not a child," Kitty said. "I think I grew up five years ago at Wynne. And you, Lion, are not a fairy tale of mine, nor are we strangers. In your heart, you know that what I am telling you is true. But you did not wait for me. How sad it is that you must wait so long for *her,* since, as I understand it, she is in mourning and you will not be able to wed for a year. You must love her, want her, very much."

Again she wondered at the viscount's little hesitation.

"I am sorry, my dear Kitty," he told her then, his voice harsh. "I would not have hurt you for the world. But I had no idea, truly, that what you felt for me was anything more than a girl's infatuation that you would soon outgrow. And I know you will, Kitty, someday you will. And then you will wonder at your actions today, and shake your head and smile at yourself. And I will come and dance at your wedding, and wish you happy, for you are very dear to me, the little sister I never had."

Kitty dashed a few angry tears from her eyes. He saw that they glowed golden in her distress, and that she was breathing hard, and he realized with a sudden stab of emotion that she had never looked so beautiful as she did now in this moment of rage and regret.

She picked up the train of her habit, and then she stood ramrod straight. "You will never dance at my wedding, Lionel Eden," she told him in a fierce little voice, "for no matter what you believe, what I feel for you is not a passing thing, a light infatuation. Dear God, Lion! I have loved you for five long years. I love you still; I will always love you. No, I shall never wed, not now."

She turned away then, and, somewhat stunned by her passion, he followed her as she went and untied her horse. Without a word, he cupped his hands and she stepped lightly up to the saddle. He smelled again the sweet warmth of her, the light perfume she wore, and he was reminded of their kiss at Deane. As she arranged her skirts, she stared down at him.

"Do you love her so much, Lion?" she asked in a whisper.

The viscount wished he could look away from her sad, accusing eyes. "We are betrothed, Kitty," he made himself say.

She closed her eyes for a moment, and then she said, "My mother told me once that you cannot *make* someone love you, no matter how hard you try. I didn't believe her then, but now I see that she was right. And even though the Dowager Duchess calls me Lady Lochinvar, all my faithfulness, my love, has been to no avail. It is too bad. And when I think how happy I was that I was a woman at last, and you were coming home to me. . . ."

She paused and took a deep breath. "I cannot, from my heart, wish you happy, Lion. Perhaps I shall be able to do so someday. For now, the pain is too intense, the wound too fresh. So I will only say good-bye."

She pulled on the reins, and he was forced to let go of the bridle. She wheeled her horse at once and cantered back the way she had come. Lionel Eden shaded his narrowed eyes with his hand as he watched her until she disappeared over a rise. He stood staring after her even then, his lips set in a hard line. She was right, of course. He had known she loved him, and, he admitted, it had even pleased him a little to think he had such power over her. But always he had thought of it as a benevolent power, for Kitty Cahill was a special young lady, and he had spoken truly when he said she was dear to him. He cursed under his breath now. He had hurt her, and there was no way he could undo that hurt.

But she is still very young, he told himself as he mounted his horse. She will recover from this passion, just as I told her she would. I am sorry, and I admit it is my fault, for I should have discouraged her long before now.

As the viscount rode slowly back to his farmers, he realized that he was ashamed of himself, and he did not care for the feeling. But he also knew he was now firmly committed to Mary Gardner, and nothing could change that. Not even Lady Catherine Cahill, with all her determination, passion, and suddenly startling beauty.

He frowned as he considered the girl that he had just seen. She had been dressed in a smart green habit that clung to every fresh, young curve. And she had looked especially beautiful to him, her eyes glowing with her intensity, and the fiery curls under her riding hat sparkling in the sunlight, as full of life as she was herself. He had even felt an instant response to her attraction, that familiar, growing warmth in his body that told him that he could want her very easily if he let himself do so. He shook his head. He was a fool, for she was not for him, not now. And somehow, he must make sure Lady Catherine forgot him, and this foolish, faithful love she had for him as well.

He waved to his farmers as he rode past them, for he needed to be alone now. Besides being ashamed, he realized he was humbled, too. Humbled to think of her devotion, no matter how sadly misplaced it was. Whoever captured Lady Catherine Cahill at last would be a lucky man. He envied him, whoever he was.

Lady Catherine was exhausted when she reached Berkeley Square again, late that afternoon. Agatha Allendon took one look at her strained, white face, the dark smudges under her eyes, and cut short her apology and explanation to send her to bed. As Kitty climbed the stairs, leaning heavily on the bannister, the dowager called after her.

"You are to rest until morning, Kitty," she ordered as the girl turned to look down at her. "There will be plenty of time then to discuss this day's events. Run along now, do, puss! I'll have a tray sent up to you, for you must be hungry."

Kitty was not a bit hungry, but she nodded, and the dowager frowned as she went back to the drawing room. She felt as if she had been talking to a pale little ghost of the girl she knew and loved. It was as if, like a fine piece of crystal, she had shattered into a million pieces under intolerable strain.

But when Kitty came down the next morning, the dowager was relieved to see that, physically at least, she had recovered completely. As she hugged both Miss Jane and Miss Eliza before she took her seat, Agatha Allendon marveled anew at the resiliency of youth. How unfortunate it is that the heart, in contrast, is so slow to mend, she thought.

Both the lady's companions made light conversation at the breakfast table, so it was not until they were alone later that the dowager learned what had transpired at Benning. She shook her head, but she did not scold Kitty for her indiscretion. She knew she would not have been able to stop her even if she had known of her plans, any more than she would have been able to stop a runaway horse. And since there was no harm done, and no one knew of the adventure, there was no reason to tell anyone about it now. Anyone at all, she told herself, a sudden picture of Lady Deane's horrified face coming to her mind.

The two sat quietly for a moment, and then Kitty said, "I find I am not much in the mood for pleasure, ma'am. And so, I hope you will forgive me if I ask permission to go home. I—I do not think I could bear to remain and watch them together. Not now."

The dowager nodded. "Yes, perhaps that would be best, my dear. But do stay aweek or two. You will not have to see the viscount, for he remains at Benning for some time."

Kitty rose and curtsied. "Very well, ma'am," she said, her voice composed. "I must admit, I would not be averse to making this Miss Gardner's acquaintance. I would see for myself the paragon who stole my Lion away."

The dowager was not at all sure of the wisdom of such a meeting, but when she saw how composed Kitty was in the days that followed, she relented, and began to plan a small dinner party.

However, before the evening of it arrived, Kitty made the lady's acquaintance, quite unplanned. She had been driving in the park with the dowager when that lady suddenly ordered her coachman to halt. Kitty watched her as she beckoned to a dark-haired lady who was strolling between two gentlemen. As the lady smiled and nodded, and walked toward the carriage, Kitty knew this was Viscount Benning's betrothed, even before the dowager whispered that information. She studied her carefully.

Throughout the introductions, she forced herself to remain cool and collected. With Miss Gardner was her uncle, a Mr. George Gardner, and someone introduced as her second cousin, Mr. Franklin Dedham. Kitty barely spared them a glance. Instead, she was taking stock of the woman smiling up at her. Even dressed in mourning, she was lovely, and her smile was warm and sincere. And when she spoke, her gentle voice was soft and musical.

"How delightful to make your acquaintance at last, Lady Catherine," she said. "The viscount has told me so much about you—indeed, about all his family."

Beside her, the lady's uncle coughed behind his hand. Kitty glanced at him quickly. He was an older man with a sallow complexion, and since he had removed his high-crowned beaver, she could see he was almost completely bald. He did not look as if he had a very pleasant disposition, for the frequent frowns he must have indulged in over the years were etched now in permanent lines on his lean face. Beside him, the younger man grinned at her somewhat vacuously, and

Kitty wondered if he had all his wits. Mr. Dedham was short and stout, with round cheeks and soft, baby-fine brown hair. He had little eyes set rather too close together, and a florid complexion. She judged him to be in his late thirties, and she did not envy Miss Gardner her companions at all.

The dowager did not keep her horses standing for long. After asking Miss Gardner to call some morning soon, she gave her coachman the office to start. Kitty said good-bye, even smiled a little as the carriage moved away, but inside, she felt as if she were bleeding. And when the dowager questioned her, all she could do was shake her head and bite her lip.

But seated in the dowager's library a short time later, she was more forthcoming when that lady asked for her opinion.

"Miss Gardner is very lovely, just as you said, your grace," Kitty told her. "Lovely, well mannered, and gracious. A paragon, indeed."

Agatha Allendon nodded. "She is that, Kitty. But how unfortunate she is in her relations! There was something I could not like about that Mr. Gardner . . ."

Her voice faded away, and Kitty said, "Yes, and I, myself, wonder if that cousin of hers is not a bit feeble-minded, ma'am."

The dowager shook her head. "How unfortunate it is that one cannot choose their relatives, is it not, dear Kitty? Why, if that were the case, I am sure there would be so many changes made in every family in England, that we would all be at sixes and sevens for the longest time!"

Kitty assured her she would never, ever wish to change her, which pleased the old lady a great deal.

The two sat and chatted of other things then, but when Kitty excused herself, she referred again to the viscount's fiancée.

Just before she left the library, she paused, and turned back. The dowager saw her eyes were full of pain, and she put out her hand. "Do you know what is quite the most awful thing about this of all, ma'am?" she asked.

Agatha Allendon waited, holding her breath. Kitty sighed and shook her head.

"I *liked* her," she said in a dead little voice. "I didn't want to. I wanted to hate her. But she is good and kind and she will make Lion a wonderful wife. A much better wife than I would, I am sure. But how much easier it would be for me to bear this if she were horrid—selfish or vain, or ill-tempered!"

Ten

LADY CATHERINE CAHILL joined the ranks of the debutantes who were presented in the spring of 1816. True, she was only just seventeen, and any other mother would have insisted that her daughter wait another year before permitting her to enter society with all its dangers and pitfalls. But Lady Deane had come to see, after a long discussion with the Dowager Duchess of Wynne at Christmastime, that Kitty was better launched as soon as it could be arranged.

"For you have seen for yourself, Rose," the dowager had said. "It is very plain that she has not forgotten the viscount, not even to the smallest degree."

"But she accepts his loss now, ma'am," Rose Cahill pointed out. "She is calm and resigned."

"Very true," the dowager agreed. Then, bending closer, she whispered, "But the sooner we can introduce her to other men, keep her busy with a whirl of activity—balls and parties and flirtations—the better. She is much too quiet now, and there is such a lost look in those handsome eyes of hers. I pray she will meet someone this spring, someone who can make her forget. For even if she never loves anyone as she has loved Lionel, young bodies have their own way of demanding satisfaction and completion."

Lady Deane's complexion had reddened at this indelicate, frank speaking, but she had had to admit the old lady had a point. Kitty was not the type of girl to be happy, celibate. She had too much passion, too many banked fires smoldering inside, to shun the marital state forever.

"What news of the viscount, ma'am?" she had asked next. "Has the date for the wedding been set?"

Agatha Allendon had shaken her head. "No, and it puzzles me," she had said slowly. "Miss Gardner continues to reside with her relatives, and although Lionel is very attentive when he comes to town, he is more often at Benning. Of course, Miss Gardner cannot attend social events as yet, for she has not put off her blacks." She sniffed. "Her uncle and that cousin of hers are still in London as well. One wonders why they do not return to Jamaica, but perhaps they intend to remain until their kinswoman is safely wed."

"Someone told me the young lady is very wealthy," Rose Cahill volunteered. "That might be their concern."

The dowager had nodded a little. "Yes, she has a fortune, that is true. And she is a lovely young woman, gracious and loving and kind. In spite of my love for Kitty, and my regrets for her, I must admit I have grown fond of Miss Gardner. It is too bad!"

But later, back at Deane, when she was told of the treat in store for her, Kitty had a hard time looking suitably excited. She realized that she did not care very much if she ever made her comeout now.

When she had returned home the previous autumn, she had taken up her old occupations as calmly as she could. Of course there had been a painful session with her mother when that good woman learned of the viscount's betrothal, but since that time, his name had seldom been mentioned. Even Emery Cahill had learned to keep any news of the man to himself, after his mother had had a quiet word with him. And no plans had been made to go to Wynne at Christmas until Lady Deane had received word that the viscount would not be attending the festivities that year. Instead, he had invited Miss Gardner and her relatives to celebrate the holidays at Benning.

As had become their custom, the Deanes arrived in London late in April. Lady Deane made sure Kitty was so busy, she did not have a moment to brood. A grand ballgown was bespoke, for the Cahills planned a gala evening to mark their daughter's entrance to society. And there were other gowns to choose as well, and all the many fripperies that were needed for a young lady soon to be so feted.

Kitty fell into bed exhausted many nights, and it was true it was easier for her to keep thoughts of Lionel Eden at bay, here in town.

At least it was until she saw him again. She was riding in Hyde Park with her brother and Garth Allendon, who had hastened to renew his pursuit of her the very afternoon she had arrived in town, when she saw the viscount and Miss Gardner cantering toward them. Kitty's face was composed as the two parties halted to exchange greetings. She saw that Miss Gardner was as lovely as ever, dressed now in dove gray, and her smile was as warm and genuine as she remembered. And Lionel —ah, Lion!—was as handsome as he had always been. Their eyes had met, of course, and Kitty concentrated on keeping her head high when she saw the little question in his own. They exchanged a few pleasant, innocuous words before Kitty turned away to ask Miss Gardner how she did. As she did so, she wondered if Lion had told her of her love for him. She rather thought he had not, for she could read no restraint in either Miss Gardner's expression or her conversation, and she was relieved.

She was also relieved that the encounter only lasted for a few minutes. Emery excused them, claiming another appointment. As they rode away, Kitty realized how lucky she was to have a brother who was so kind and understanding.

After that morning, she seemed to see Lionel Eden a

great deal more often than she cared to. Sometimes, she would look up at a party to find his dark blue eyes on her, a little frown between his brows. She wondered at it, not knowing the viscount was concerned for her.

For Lady Catherine Cahill had made a distinct hit with society that spring, and there were those among the gentlemen who considered her an Incomparable. Kitty thought it very strange that someone who did not give a snap of her fingers about her popularity and acceptance, should be so admired, but that was certainly the case. But perhaps it was her coolness, her lack of interest in forming any attachment, that drew the bachelors to her side so often. "At least she is a girl who is not bent on matrimony," a Mr. Kay informed his friend Lord Hadley. That young peer nodded. "And she is so handsome, so graceful, too!" he enthused.

And so Kitty's dance card was always filled, and she was sure to be surrounded by a bevy of gentlemen at any party she attended. Lionel Eden watched her whenever he could. He wished he might warn her away from Mr. Kay, who had even less money than he had sense, or tell her that the rakish Lord Deeds was no fit companion for a girl her age, being all of thirty-five and a devil with the ladies as well. Lord Deed's reputation—and intentions —were decidedly suspect. But of course, the viscount knew he could not do that. It was up to her parents and her brother to keep her safe, and caution her about her choice of companions. Strangely, however, even though he had told her she would recover from her love for him, and had hoped she would meet someone else this Season she could love and marry, now, perversely, he found he did not care to contemplate any such solution.

Not a one of them are worthy of Kitty, he told himself one evening as he stood behind his fiancée's chair, staring in Kitty's direction. To think she wastes a smile on Lord Deeds, dances so gracefully with the foolish Mr. Kay, allows Lord Hadley to fan her with every sign

of delight! Why, even Garth Allendon was making a
perfect cake of himself over Kitty! The viscount had
been sure she had better taste than to encourage every
loose screw and foolish fribble to dance attendance on
her!

Mary Gardner, looking up at him to make a quiet
remark, was stunned at the unhappy expression she saw
in his eyes, the little frown he sported. She turned back
to see who he was looking at, and then she lowered her
eyes to her lavender skirts and smoothed them with a
black-mittened hand. She could not dance, and since
that was forbidden her, neither could her fiancé. For a
moment, she wished they might join the set that was
forming. Surely it was difficult for Lionel to spend a
festive evening like this propping up a wall, and only
watching others enjoying themselves. Miss Gardner
smiled. He was such a good, wonderful man! She knew
how lucky she was to have met him.

And so she set herself to conversing with him with as
much animation as she could muster. She had the
pleasure of seeing his expression brighten, and his dark
blue eyes twinkle down at her again, and she was
relieved.

Kitty saw it as well, and her heart skipped that
familiar beat. She wished that the viscount and Miss
Gardner had not come this evening. She wished she
never had to see either one of them again, and certainly
not together where she was reminded so constantly of
her loss.

But when she lay sleepless on her bed later, and
watched the gray dawn creeping in her windows and
displacing the dark shadows of night, she knew this was
something she must learn to bear. And not only seeing
them together. Now that Miss Gardner was wearing soft
colors again, and attending parties, she knew it would
not be long before the banns were posted.

Kitty rolled over and closed her eyes. But what
difference will that make? she asked herself. Their

marriage was a foregone conclusion months ago, as you have been well aware. Perhaps it would be better for you to accept someone else's hand and have done with it, she thought. There was Garth Allendon, still so determined to marry her he asked her at least once a week. And then there was Roger Danvers, Lord Deeds. Of all her beaux, he had the most disturbing effect on her. The touch of his hand caused shivers up and down her body, and his age and sophistication, his obvious desire and admiration for her, soothed her pain. And she knew he wanted her badly. His every look had become a caress, his laughing, light conversation was full of double meaning. And he was an earl, and wealthy to boot. Yes, she told herself, she must consider Lord Deeds more carefully. For she had come to see that she did not want to remain single all her days, for such a worthless sacrifice would mean loneliness for her, and certainly nothing at all to the viscount.

And perhaps if she were married, too, looking forward to having children, managing her own home, she would be able to forget Lion at last. Her mouth twisted in a wry grimace. She knew full well she would never forget him as long as she drew breath.

And so, she could not bring herself to the sticking point, no matter how she tried. When the earl proposed a week later, at the Hadley ball, she told him she must have more time to consider it, for she had had no thought of marriage to anyone just yet.

"My dear child, how refreshing you are," the earl drawled, before he kissed her hand.

Kitty stared at his handsome blond head, the thin aristocratic face, those knowing, cool gray eyes. He winked at her.

"I do assure you I will do my utmost to see to your—um—pleasure, dear Kitty," he said.

"And to yours?" she could not help asking.

His smile broadened. "But of course, my dear. For your pleasure shall become mine, naturally. Do you know, I think it was your flaming hair that drew me first, and your wide, bewitching green eyes. You are well named, Kitty, but still, I wonder if you are not perhaps a witch, or a witch's familiar. I am sure I have never been so mesmerized in my life."

Kitty smiled a little. "I cast no spells, m'lord," she told him. "You know I don't."

"You cannot help but cast a spell, love," he said, sitting down beside her and sliding an arm around her waist. They were sitting out a dance at the time, alone in their host's library.

Kitty stared up at him gravely. "Are you going to kiss me?" she asked, her prosaic voice very curious.

The earl paused. He had been lowering his lips to hers, but now he raised his head and laughed out loud. When he could speak again, he said, "I am, indeed. And I beg you not to say another word."

Kitty closed her eyes as his lips covered hers. But although she waited rather breathlessly for that warm stirring deep inside she had known when Lion kissed her, now she felt nothing but an odd detachment, as if she were floating above the two of them, observing them passively.

The earl was frowning as he raised his head. "Are you so cold, my dear?" he whispered. "I see I have a formidable task ahead of me, but I do not despair. No, indeed. For Kitty," he went on as his long thin hand caressed her arm, "I do perceive you to be well worth my most ardent efforts. Surely that fiery head of yours is not deceiving. No, that would be impossible. You will be a passionate woman, I know. How fortunate that I know just how to go about arousing you, love."

Kitty removed his wandering hands and rose from the sofa. "That is something we shall have to see, won't we, m'lord?" she made herself say. "But for now, I think we should return to the ballroom. My mother will be wondering what has become of me, after all this time."

She waited a little breathlessly as the earl leisurely got

to his feet, a speculative look in his eyes, as if he were contemplating refusing her directive, and beginning his transformation of her at once. As she raised her chin a little in defiance, he smiled.

"Very well—for now, dear Kitty," he said, bowing to her. "But I shall call on you tomorrow, and tomorrow, and tomorrow. And every time we are alone, I shall continue your—mm—your education."

Kitty turned away from the serious, intent look he gave her, to walk steadily to the door.

As the earl took her arm to escort her back to Lady Deane, she saw Lionel Eden crossing the hall. His face darkened when he noticed that they had just left the library, and that there were no other guests with them. Kitty had the strangest feeling that the viscount wanted to speak to her, but he did not. He only bowed as they passed him. Lord Deeds waved a careless hand before he bent over Kitty to whisper to her again.

Sometime after the supper dance, when she was returning to the ballroom alone, Kitty saw Lionel Eden approaching her. He wore a look of determination, and she was not surprised when he asked if he might have a moment of her time. She looked around. Miss Gardner was deep in conversation with their hostess, and her own mother was enjoying a visit with some old friends. Kitty shrugged, trying for nonchalance even though her heart was beating at a rapid rate.

"Why, of course, m'lord," she said, hoping he could not tell how unnerved she was at being close to him again.

To her astonishment, the viscount took her arm and led her to a small antechamber nearby. It was quite deserted, and, after they had entered, he shut the door behind them with a resounding snap.

"Whatever are you doing, sir?" Kitty asked, bewildered. "You know it is not at all the thing for us to be private like this."

"Did you object to being private with Lord Deeds earlier?" the viscount asked, putting his hands on her shoulders to turn her toward him. Kitty stared up at him, startled by the anger she saw in his dark blue eyes.

Suddenly his hands tightened. "Puss, puss!" he said, shaking his head. "You must not let that man dance attendance on you; you must not encourage him! He is not for you! He is in no way worthy of you! His reputation, his escapades and affairs—why, you are too fine for the likes of him."

"And just what right do you have to tell me this, Lion?" Kitty demanded.

"I know I have no right," the viscount said, his jaw firm. "But I have waited for your mother or your brother to do so, and it is obvious that they have not. Therefore I took it upon myself—"

Suddenly, Kitty tore away from his grasp, and moved back a few steps, her green eyes blazing. "You took too much upon yourself, m'lord," she told him. "What I do, whom I see, is none of your concern. Not now. Not any more."

She saw the viscount's cheekbones redden, and she felt a stab of triumph. "But since you are so interested in my affairs, I will tell you that I am contemplating marriage to the earl," she went on. "He asked me this very evening."

She was forced to retreat before the dark anger that came over the viscount's face, and he stalked her. As he grasped her arms again, he shook her, hard.

"No! You must not do such a thing, Kitty!" he said through gritted teeth. "He will make you miserable with his excesses, his lack of honor. Oh, he woos you now with considerable address, I am sure, but in a little while he will tire of you as he has tired of so many others, and he will leave you to your own devices. I know the man; you must believe me!"

"You are hurting me, m'lord," Kitty managed to say

as this impassioned speech ended. "If you do not stop, I shall have bruises there tomorrow. Bruises I would find very difficult to explain to my mother."

Lionel Eden released her, and she took a deep breath. "Besides, the earl's behavior will not bother me," she told him, trying for a calm, reasonable tone. "You see, I do not love him. But since I have come to agree with you that marriage is my only recourse, sir, it might just as well be to him as anyone."

"Kitty, dear girl!" Lion cried. "You have no idea what you are letting yourself in for! Marriage is not a casual thing, it lasts a lifetime. Listen to me! Please wait! You are still so very young, why, there are years yet before you should choose a husband. And in those years, you will come to see—"

Lady Catherine stamped her foot and shook her fist at him. "Young! *Young!* Why do you continually prate about my age, m'lord? I am not young, except in years. And since I know full well that I shall never love anyone ever again, why shouldn't I marry where I please? The earl is charming and amusing and wealthy. And he will understand better than a Garth Allendon or a Mr. Kay when he realizes I have no love for him. Indeed, I begin to think we will deal very well together, even better than I thought we would. For since I do not love him, he cannot hurt me, don't you see?"

She paused when she saw the look on Lionel Eden's face. He was staring at her as if he had never seen her before. She waited, but he had nothing further to say, and she tossed her head.

"Silenced at last, m'lord?" she asked, her voice only shaking a little. "Well, that is something to be thankful for. And I thank you for your advice, of course," she added, dropping him a little curtsy. "But what the Lady Catherine Cahill chooses to do is none of your concern. Not now, and not ever again. You decided your future, the way you would go. Do me the kindness of allowing me to decide mine."

She stared at him, hiding her love for him behind an arrogant look. She saw him shake his handsome head, and how his mouth twisted in a grimace of—of pain?—distress? She did not know. She only knew she had vanquished him, and she wondered that the victory should taste so bitter on her tongue.

They stood together a moment more, and then Lionel Eden bowed. "You must allow me to escort you back to the ballroom, Lady Catherine," he said, holding out his arm. As they left the room together, neither said a word. But just before he left her, he put his other hand over hers where it rested on his arm, and, looking down at her, he whispered, "Think well before you act, Kitty. Think very well. I would not have you hurt."

Kitty's gaze was steady. "How strange to hear *you* say such thing, m'lord," she said softly. "Especially when you were the one who hurt me so badly just a few months ago."

She heard the viscount's sharp, indrawn breath, and she drew her hand away. "Give you good evening, sir," she said.

"Very well, Kitty," he said slowly. "But do not think I will let you destroy yourself quite so easily. For even if you do not heed my advice, be sure I shall have a quiet word with your brother or your mother. I do assure you you will not be allowed to marry the earl after all."

Kitty gave him a speaking glance before she moved away, her head held high. After only a few steps, she was surrounded by her admirers, all clamoring for her attention, and demanding to know where she had been hiding herself. The viscount turned his back on the group to return to his fiancée.

He made no attempt to speak to any of the Cahills that evening, but the very next day he made a point of seeking out his old friend, Emery Cahill. He told him of his concerns even though he felt very uncomfortable doing so. Kitty's brother stared at him in disbelief, although he made no comment until the viscount finished speaking.

"I—I thank you, Lion," he said at last. "I know that you are right. But I do not think Kitty is even thinking of marriage, most certainly not to the earl. M'father would deny the man if he should dare to ask for her hand, of that you may be sure."

Emery's forehead wrinkled in a frown then. "But—but why do you take it on yourself to tell me this?" he asked, his voice stiff. The viscount could tell he had not forgotten Kitty's supposed love for himself, and that he was not at ease with him anymore because of it.

"Emery, no matter what your family thinks, I did not lead Kitty on," he made himself say. "I was as surprised as you no doubt were, when she told me she loved me. But although I do not love her that way, she is still as dear to me as my own sister would be, and I cannot see her hurt."

During this earnest and heartfelt speech, Emery Cahill's open face had cleared a little, and now he clapped his old friend on the shoulder. "Thank you for telling me that, Lion," he said. "I cannot tell you how awkward it has been for me, for you are my good friend. But Kitty was so hurt, so—so destroyed. Now I know that it was not your fault. I can be easy. And I hope you will understand why I cannot continue to see you under the circumstances."

Lionel Eden grinned at him. "I do. And someday, when my Miss Kittycat falls in love and marries, as she will, you and I can cry friends again. I look forward to it, for I have missed you."

Emery shook his head. "And I, you! But I beg you to stop worrying about the earl. M'father is more than a match for him."

Lionel Eden did not allow himself to feel relieved at these optimistic words. Instead, he went to call on the Dowager Duchess of Wynne as soon as he left Emery Cahill.

He found her just descending from her landau after a shopping trip with her two companions. As he helped her up the steps of her house, he asked if he might have a moment of her time.

"As many as you like, dear boy," she told him, waving Miss Jane and Miss Eliza away.

She took him into the drawing room, and, after ordering them both a glass of wine and then telling her butler she was not to be disturbed, she took her seat and peered up at him expectantly. "There is something amiss, Lionel?" she asked. "How may I help you?"

"It is not for myself I ask, ma'am," the viscount told her. He stared down into his wine, as if seeking for a way there to recount his difficulties. Agatha Allendon waited patiently.

"You see, I have not been able to help noticing the company Lady Catherine Cahill is keeping these days," he said at last. "And I am sure you must agree with me that the idiots she allows to dance attendance on her are not at all worthy of the honor. Besides, she has captured the Earl of Deeds's eye. You know the man. I am sure I do not have to tell you that any liaison between him and Kitty Cahill is not to be thought of."

The dowager sat calmly, not a ripple of the exultation she was feeling inside showing on her wrinkled face. Being a good deal older and wiser than others, it never crossed her mind to ask why the viscount should take this matter into his own hands; why he was so concerned for Kitty. But she wondered, for the first time, if Lionel was happy in his engagement. It seemed very strange to her that a man, supposedly mad with love for one woman, would put himself to the trouble of bothering about another's affairs. Could it be that Lionel felt more than mere kinship for Kitty Cahill after all? But what then of the lovely Miss Gardner?

Putting these thoughts aside to be pondered later, she cleared her throat and said, "I quite agree with you, dear boy. I, too, have been puzzled by Kitty. But you

must have seen how popular she is! No doubt it has
gone to her head a bit. As for the questionable earl,
there is no danger of marriage there. He is just amusing
himself, but he cannot have Kitty, nor can he hurt her.''

"Oh, yes he can!" the viscount said grimly. "She told
me last evening at the Hadley ball, that the earl had
asked her to marry him. More, she said she was
considering it seriously."

The dowager's brows rose in disbelief. So Lionel had
spoken to Kitty, alone, had he? Taxed her with her
behavior? Chastised her for her choice of companions
and admirers? Better and better!

"I shall have a word with her mother, Lionel," she
said now. "And a word with that young lady herself,"
she added sternly. "We want none of *his* stamp in the
family, no indeed!"

"I am relieved to hear you say so, ma'am," the
viscount told her. "But I fear you may have a harder
time to it than you think. Kitty—Lady Catherine, that
is—has changed out of all recognition. Why, I found it
hard to believe she is the same girl I used to know. She
has grown cold and arrogant, with a kind of careless
indifference."

He paused, and put his glass down on the table by his
side before he rose to pace the room, frowning as he did
so. The dowager waited, holding her breath.

"Indeed, she told me it did not matter whom she
married now, and so the earl would do very well," he
went on at last, his words sounding strangled. "But
Kitty—and that devil! No, no, it must not be!"

"And I am sure it will never be," the dowager interrupted, firmly repressing the "Aha!" that she longed to
utter. "You make too much of the matter, Lionel. Kitty
is young. And she is feeling a little cocky, perhaps, at
the power she had just discovered she has over the
opposite sex. But she will not marry him. She is only
seventeen, remember."

The viscount nodded, but as he took his seat again, he

mused, "Strange how easy it is to forget that, isn't it? For Kitty seems much older. She always has."

Wisely, the dowager changed the subject then, although she admitted it took a great deal of will power for her to do so. "How is Miss Gardner keeping these days, Lionel?" she asked. "I have not seen her lately. And I have been meaning to ask her when she will put off her mourning, and when your marriage is to take place."

The viscount did not look at her as he replied, "Mary is well, thank you, ma'am. I expect we will be making final plans in a month or so. There is no hurry, after all."

The dowager's brows rose again. Surely for such a virile young man as the viscount, this had been a long and tedious engagement, she thought.

Lionel Eden took his leave a few minutes later. He left a very pensive dowager duchess behind him, and that lady remained deep in thought for some time.

And how surprised she would have been if she could have followed Lionel Eden through the London streets to his next destination. For the viscount made his way to the Admiralty, where he spent some time with one of the officers he had become acquainted with in the previous months, having a serious discussion about the whereabouts of one of His Majesty's frigates.

Eleven

THAT EVENING, the viscount and his fiancée attended a dance given by Lady Booth at her house in Portman Square. It was a perfect crush, but even so, Lionel Eden spotted Lady Catherine Cahill almost at once. She was dressed in an emerald green gown that exposed a great deal more soft white skin than he considered seemly. He also noticed how it clung to every one of her curves, and he wondered what Lady Deane was thinking of to allow her daughter to appear so immodestly dressed. He did not notice that every other young lady in the room was similarly attired.

As he seated Miss Gardner in a place where she could watch the dancing and sat down beside her, the viscount never took his eyes from the slender, shapely, red-haired sprite who was attracting so much attention. Mr. Kay was holding her hand and laughing down at her, while on her other side, Lord Hadley begged for her regard. The viscount's frown deepened when he saw Lord Deeds stroll up and make some remark as he raised his quizzing glass for a complete, leisurely inspection of the young lady. Kitty made a face at him before she pirouetted and curtsied. The viscount's hands that were resting on his knees tightened into two fists.

Mary Gardner followed his gaze as before. She was not surprised to see that it was the lovely Lady Catherine he watched, for she had noticed in the past how often his eyes rested on her. A little frown creased Miss Gardner's smooth white brow.

As the lady they both watched tapped Lord Deed's arm with her fan in mock reproof and laughed up at him, Miss Gardner said, "She is very beautiful, is she not?"

The viscount did not bother to turn to her. "Who is?" he asked gruffly.

"Why, Lady Catherine Cahill, of course," his fiancée said. "And she is so spirited, so gay, is she not?"

The viscount saw Lord Deeds put his hand on Kitty's bare shoulder, and he stiffened. "Too spirited, and a great deal too free with her favors," he said. "She should be spanked."

"Ah, she is only very young. I am sure there is no vice in her," Miss Gardner said. "You have known her for some time, haven't you, Lionel?" she asked next.

The viscount turned his head at last, to give his fiancée his complete attention. "Yes, all my life," he said. "We are distant cousins, and I watched her grow up." His dark blue eyes began to twinkle. "What a funny little thing she was, Mary, when she was small! All scrawny arms and legs and wide green eyes. In fact, her eyes always looked too big for the rest of her. And how she used to follow Emery and me around, trying her best to match our feats." He chuckled. "All she got for her pains were a great many bumps, bruises, and scrapes, not that that ever stopped her. I used to call her my little Miss Kittycat."

"Emery is her brother?" Miss Gardner asked, interrupting his remembrances.

"Yes, and my dear friend. While I was in Jamaica, he took over the care of Benning for me, so it would not suffer in my absence."

He saw the little frown in her eyes, and how her face paled, and he took her hands and held them between his own, big warm ones. "Do not look so, my dear," he whispered, bending closer. "That is all behind you now. Trust me. You will come to no harm."

Miss Gardner smiled up at him, and although it was not one of her better efforts, it seemed to reassure him. "I know, and all thanks to you, Lionel," she said. "I cannot tell you how grateful I am that we met, and you were so understanding, so caring."

Lady Catherine Cahill tried to ignore the sight of the viscount whispering to Mary Gardner and holding her hands in his by turning her back to them. She was grateful when the orchestra began to play just then, and she could take the earl's arm to join the first set.

She was not the only one who was observing the engaged couple that evening. The Dowager Duchess of Wynne, accompanied by her two companions, had honored the party, and now, Miss Jane told her everything that was happening across the room.

The dowager frowned. "I simply do not understand it at all," she said. "For if Lionel is so attentive, so in love with Miss Gardner, why on earth is he fretting over Kitty's behavior?"

"Perhaps it is only that he is fond of her as he said, after all, ma'am," Miss Eliza suggested.

The dowager snorted. "That may be, but I still have my doubts that that is all he feels for her, even now. No, but I do see we must be patient. Still, my dears, I think it would be a good thing if you could find out as much as you can about Miss Mary Gardner, and her two relatives. Maybe you can strike up an acquaintance with this cousin, Hetty Dedham, that she is staying with in town, and learn more of her that way."

Both middle-aged ladies nodded, their eyes brightening at the thought of future investigations. And when Miss Jane saw Miss Dedham talking to some people nearby, she was quick to excuse herself so she might join them. The dowager smiled. Whatever would I do without Jane and Eliza? she asked herself, knowing that

if there were anything at all in the girl's past, they would
discover it in short order.

She forgot the lady, however, when she saw Kitty
dancing nearby. And when she saw that she was
partnered by the rakish earl, her lips tightened. Even
with her failing eyesight, she could see how intimate he
was, how his hands seemed to caress Kitty's skin, how
he whispered to her as they danced, and she resolved to
speak to Lady Catherine Cahill tomorrow. She admitted
she was concerned. She had not thought Kitty would
encourage any man, but it seemed she had been wrong.
And there was a new, almost reckless air about the girl,
as if she did not care what happened to her anymore.
And that would never do. Agatha Allendon sighed, suddenly feeling very old and tired. But she would see that
Kitty came to no harm in spite of all her wild, careless
passion, if it was the last thing she did.

She was relieved to see, as the evening wore on, that
the girl only danced twice with the earl, and that she
remained in the ballroom, not allowing him to see her
alone. And she was further relieved when she noticed
Kitty smiling and laughing with others. To anyone who
did not know of the situation, it would appear that she
was having a wonderful time. But the dowager knew
there was more than a tinge of desperate abandon in her
laugh and her behavior, and that she was volatile as
gunpowder.

Later, Miss Eliza told her that a Mr. Kendall, who
had just returned from India, seemed much taken with
Kitty, and that Lord Deeds did not appear to like it.

The dowager knew of Paul Kendall. Although not of
the peerage, he came from an old, respected family. He
was a man in his middle twenties, and he was steady and
reliable. He was also handsome, with raven-dark hair,
gray eyes, and clean-cut features. If Kitty had not fallen
in love with Lionel Eden, the dowager would have
thought Mr. Kendall a perfect mate for her. She
wondered if Kitty could be persuaded to consider him at

some future date? He would be so good for her!

Kitty would have been astounded if she had been privy to the dowager's thoughts. Lord Hadley had introduced her to the new gentleman at his request, and although she agreed he was handsome and personable, she felt no more for him than she did for any of her admirers. But looking up and catching the viscount watching her, she made herself smile and flirt with him. Mr. Kendall appeared to be entranced.

The following morning, the dowager sent a message around the square asking Lady Catherine to call on her that same afternoon. Since the Season had begun, she had not seen as much of the girl as she would have liked, for Kitty was like a whirlwind, busy with all her new friends and endless amusements. Now, as she entered the drawing room and curtsied before she came to give her old friend a hug, the dowager was startled. Up close, she could see the strain in those wide green eyes, their reckless glitter. And she could see that under the smart primrose afternoon gown, Kitty was thinner, and as taut as a finely tuned violin string.

"How good it is to see you, ma'am," the girl said as she took a seat. Then she sighed, and put her head on the back of the chair. "And this is so restful, too," she went on. "I never seem to have a moment to myself anymore."

"So I have noticed," the dowager said, keeping her voice mild. "You are in perpetual motion. But, my dear, you must have a care lest you become ill with all your activities. You should schedule some time to be alone, to rest."

Although she nodded, Kitty did not reply. She knew full well why such a course of action was unappealing to her. For when she was alone, she could only think of Lionel Eden, and the great loss she had suffered. It was only when she was involved in parties, or flirting with a handsome beau, that she could forget him. As she knew she had to forget him. So she did not tell the dear old dowager that after her visit here, she was engaged to drive in the park with Lord Hadley, then take tea with Garth Allendon, and that she had promised to attend not one, but two parties that evening as well.

"There was some special reason you wished to see me, your grace?" she asked now, remembering that Lord Hadley was to take her up only thirty minutes from now.

"There was indeed, puss," the dowager said, sitting up straighter and looking stern now. "It has come to my attention that you are encouraging Lord Deeds. It will not do, Kitty. The man has an unsavory reputation, and there must be no alliance between you."

She saw Kitty lean forward, her eyes beginning to blaze with anger, and she went on, raising one hand to ensure the girl's silence. "Yes, you are quite right, Lionel told me. I had noticed you with Lord Deeds myself, but I thought you were merely amusing yourself. But Lionel tells me he has asked you to marry him, and that you are considering it. I absolutely forbid such a union, Kitty, and I suggest you cut the connection at once. I know you do not care a ha'penny for the man, so it will cause you no heartache to do so. Besides, you will hardly miss him, you have so many beaux."

As she finished speaking, she saw that Kitty had clenched her hands into fists. "And what right has Lion to come to you carrying tales, ma'am?" she asked, her voice quickening with anger. "He is much too officious! And it is none of his business what I do, as I told him myself."

"But as the head of the family, puss, it is *my* business," the dowager told her. "Pray you will not claim that *I* am too officious?"

Kitty made herself smile. "Never you, my dear friend," she said. Then she rose to pace the room with quick, nervous steps. "But, after all, what difference does it make whom I marry, ma'am?" she asked.

"Lord Deeds is well-to-do, and an earl, and he is amusing. Besides, he is everywhere received."

"He is a devil, as you would find out to your regret, my dear," the dowager retorted. "There are things I could tell you about him that would horrify you. No, Kitty, put him from your mind. For even though, having lost the viscount, you do not think it matters what happens to you, others are not so careless about your future. And so you will not be allowed to destroy yourself, going to hell in a handbasket as Lord Deeds's wife. I shall see to that!"

She stared at Lady Catherine, her dim eyes stern, and Kitty made herself laugh. "Very well, ma'am, I shall do as you say. Oh, perhaps not give him the cut direct—how unfair to the earl!—but I will not accept his proposal. There, are you satisfied now, ma'am?"

As she took her seat again, the dowager nodded. "You are a good girl, Kitty," she said.

"Perhaps I shall encourage Paul Kendall," Kitty went on. "I met him last evening, and he is very pleasant, very handsome."

"And infinitely more suitable," the dowager agreed. "But if I might make a suggestion . . . ?"

As she hesitated, Kitty's brows rose. It was most unlike the dowager to ask permission to suggest anything, especially of her. She nodded, her green eyes never leaving that wrinkled old face. "But of course you may, ma'am," she said.

"Then I suggest that you put matrimony from your mind for some time, Kitty," the dowager said, her voice serious. "You are very young, and you have been hurt. To marry coldly, without any regard at all, would be a mistake." She saw that Kitty would have replied, and she went on quickly, "Yes, my dear faithful Lady Lochinvar, I know you think you will never love again, and that may well be the case. And you have said it doesn't matter whom you wed, not now. But I would

ask you to wait for a year or two. There is something—
something—but I cannot tell you of it right now, so I
ask you to take my word for it. Wait, Kitty, wait."

Lady Catherine was puzzled. What was this "something" the dowager spoke of? Something to do with
Lionel? Miss Gardner? But that could not be. She had
seen them together last evening, smiling and deep in
conversation. She had watched Lion take the lady's
hands in his and hold them as he whispered to her, and
she had seen Mary Gardner's warm, answering smile,
the tender love she had for him shining on her face.

The mantel clock struck the hour, and Kitty jumped
to her feet. "Very well, dear ma'am, I shall wait as you
suggest," she said as she went to the mirror to adjust her
saucy bonnet. "But now I must leave you. I am to drive
with Lord Hadley, who is no doubt waiting for me even
now. You do not object to Lord Hadley, I pray?" she
added, putting on an anxious look.

The dowager snorted. "Be off with you, and do not
think to tease me, you impertinent puss," she said.
"Percy Hadley is an idiot, and you know it. You are in
no danger from him, however, for he only intends to
worship you from afar, as he worships every Season's
Incomparable. No, my dear, you might try your most
seductive wiles, but it would be to no avail. Lord Hadley
will be a bachelor when he is eighty. He is not the marrying kind."

Kitty laughed. "But how lowering, ma'am," she said
as she curtsied. "To think I shall have to watch him
make up to some new young thing next Season. I swear
it will break my heart!"

She blew the dowager a kiss before she left the room,
laughing as she did so.

The dowager smiled, and chuckled to herself as the
door closed behind her. Kitty was pert and quick, a
delight to her always. She prayed that all would come
right for her someday.

And then she wondered if she should tell Lionel Eden

that the girl had promised not to accept Lord Deeds. As she rose to go and find her companions, she decided she would not do so. Let him fret a little more, she told herself, wondering why the thought of him doing so was so very satisfying.

She saw Miss Gardner with her uncle and cousin the following afternoon. They were strolling in the park, and the dowager stopped her carriage and asked them to join her for a turn. She wondered why Miss Gardner seemed to hesitate, even as her uncle accepted with a sour little bow. Mr. Dedham giggled as he took his seat beside Mary Gardner, and the dowager noticed how she drew her skirts away from any contact with him.

"I hope you are enjoying yourself in London, sir?" she asked Mr. George Gardner.

"It is most amusing," he said in the harsh voice that sounded anything but amused.

"I am surprised that you and your nephew remain for so long, however," the dowager said next. "But perhaps I have been misinformed? I understood you own an extensive plantation in Jamaica. Surely it must need your supervision."

"I have a good overseer, your grace," Mr. Gardner told her. "And I feel my place is beside my niece, since my sister-in-law's death. I am her guardian."

"How good of you," the dowager said, her voice noncommittal.

"And you, sir, are you also enjoying your stay in England?" she asked Mr. Dedham.

Franklin Dedham looked to his uncle before he answered, for all the world as if he were asking permission to speak. "Very nice, my, my, very nice, indeed," he said at last. Then he giggled and covered his mouth with his hand. The dowager noticed he jiggled his foot almost continually, and how his close-set eyes watered in some secret delight. Clearly, Mr. Dedham was a half-wit.

Miss Gardner spoke up then, commenting on the

pleasant spring day. This afternoon she was wearing a gown of pale blue, with a modest straw bonnet. The dowager smiled at her.

"I see you have put off your mourning, my dear. I am so glad," she said. "Surely we can all look forward to wedding bells in a short time?" she asked.

Miss Gardner seemed startled, although the dowager could not be sure, for she had lowered her eyes so quickly to her neat kid gloves, to smooth them.

"Lionel has been making plans," she said in her gentle voice. "But he is busy at Benning, and he does not feel he can leave it just now. And since he has promised me a grand wedding tour, in fact, insists on it, we plan to wait until fall."

Beside her, Mr. Gardner harumped and shifted in his seat, and the dowager was amazed. He did not appear to be very happy with his niece's future husband, and for the life of her, she could not understand why. Lionel was of the peerage; he was handsome and kind and good. What was there about him that Mr. Gardner could not like? Did he perhaps object to his lack of a fortune? the dowager wondered, even as she continued to chat of innocuous things until the time came to set her visitors down.

She forgot the disapproving Mr. Gardner and his impossible nephew as soon as she saw Lady Catherine Cahill and her escort a few minutes later. Kitty was riding a chestnut mare, and she was dressed in a smart black habit, the top of which was cut like a man's riding jacket. At her throat and wrists there was a spill of white lace, and her only color was her fiery hair and green eyes. She was accompanied by Paul Kendall on a roan gelding. At the dowager's wave, Kitty trotted her mount up to the carriage to introduce Mr. Kendall to her old friend. Agatha Allendon liked him immediately. He was pleasant and witty, and from the way his eyes so often admired the girl at his side, considerably attracted to her.

As the two took their leave some moments later, the dowager saw Lord Deeds driving by in a high-perch phaeton. He was alone, except for his tiger, and even the dowager could see his sudden frown, the arrested expression on his thin, haughty face as he caught sight of Kitty's escort. He does not appear to care for any competition, the dowager told herself, and then she smiled as she ordered her coachman to start. How glad I am that he will discover, and very shortly too, that even if there had been no handsome young man to vie for Kitty's hand, she still had no intention of becoming his countess. And good riddance to the man! she thought.

When she returned to Berkeley Square, she discovered that both Miss Jane and Miss Eliza had gone to take tea with Hetty Dedham, and she ordered a tea tray for herself as she waited for them to come home. They had made short work of forming an acquaintance with the lady, and she knew it would not be long before every known fact about Miss Mary Gardner was laid out for their perusal. And then we shall see, the dowager thought as she poured out a steaming cup and reached for the sugar. For I feel, deep down in my bones, that all is not as it appears on the surface here.

At that moment, Hetty Dedham was regaling her new friends with a complete description of Mary's circumstances. Thus, in very short order indeed, they learned all about the young lady's fortune, the unfortunate death of her mother from the fever that had swept Jamaica during her stay there, and of the viscount's proposal.

"It was just like a fairy tale!" Miss Dedham enthused, bouncing a little on the striped settee in her drawing room. She was a round little woman with twinkling brown eyes, and fortunately, she loved a good gossip. "Why, just before my dear cousin Anne passed on, she agreed to the wedding, saying she could die happy knowing Mary would be so well taken care of."

"But surely her uncle would have taken care of her?" Miss Eliza remarked.

Miss Dedham frowned and looked away. "Well, yes, of course, but as I understand it from Mary, Anne did not want her daughter to remain in Jamaica with her uncle and cousin. I am sure I do not wonder at it. I know I should not say so, but George is a most unpleasant fellow to live with, and as for Franklin, well! I am afraid the boy does not have much in his brain box, you know," she whispered, leaning forward as she did so. "It is most unfortunate, for he is George's only heir. Indeed, George wrote to me once and said he had great hopes that Franklin and Mary might marry some day. I cannot tell you how relieved I was, at least, that that never came to pass. I would not wish the man on my worst enemy, no indeed!"

"It must be difficult for you to entertain them all this time," Miss Jane said.

Miss Dedham sighed. "They are not the most congenial of houseguests, that is true," she admitted. "Oh, I should not say that, and I hope I know my duty, but . . ." She sighed again. "However, they will be leaving as soon as the banns are posted."

"It must have been quite a whirlwind affair—the courtship, I mean," Miss Eliza prodded.

"Truly like a fairy tale," Miss Jane chimed in.

"Oh, the viscount swept Mary right off her feet," Miss Dedham agreed, a happy little smile playing over her face at the thought of such a tempestuous wooing. "It seems George had no idea they even knew each other, although his land adjoins Lord Benning's uncle's plantation. He was much amazed when informed of the engagement. I am sure I do not know why he says it is a pity it ever took place, that if Anne had died before she gave her permission, he, as Mary's guardian, would have refused to consider it."

She leaned closer, and her guests did likewise as she whispered, "He even said that Mary appeared to be attracted to the most unsuitable men, although, of course, the viscount cannot be considered in *that* light!" she added quickly, remembering that Lionel Eden was related in some way to the two ladies she was entertaining.

"I wonder why he would say that?" Miss Jane asked, her eyes round. "There have been other suitors?"

"Only one, several years ago. A man Mary knew from her childhood. But her uncle, even her mother, refused to allow them to marry. He was only a lieutenant in the Royal Navy, a man of no wealth or connections; a mere nobody. Such a mismatch would never do, no indeed!"

"How sad," Miss Eliza mourned. "How sad that young lovers must be parted only because of lineage and their acceptance by the *ton.*"

"But all's well that ends well, Miss Eliza," Miss Dedham told her. "For just see how it has answered! Mary is engaged to the viscount now, and although she is not a volatile girl, she appears well satisfied with her choice. So you see, older heads do know best, for if her family had not insisted she give Lieutenant Wadley up, she would be poor now, and left alone most of the time, raising a family in some unsavory location."

Neither Miss Jane nor Miss Eliza corrected this pitiful picture by pointing out that for a young lady of Miss Mary Gardner's wealth, there was no need for her to live in a hovel and do her own washing, with howling babies hanging on her skirts.

Instead, they chatted of other things, and, when a further meeting had been arranged, took their leave.

They reported everything they had learned to the dowager at dinner that evening, but she did not seem to be reassured by their report. "For even if there was another man at one time, it is obvious that she has forgotten him, my dears," she told them. "Otherwise, she would never have accepted Lionel's proposal."

"I am sure Viscount Benning could make any woman

forget another man," Miss Eliza said loyally. "He is so handsome, so good and gay!"

"Not as gay as he used to be," the dowager remarked, as if to herself. "Well," she said more briskly, "do continue to cultivate Miss Dedham, my friends. There may still be something to be learned from her. For I am sure that there is something strange in all this that we do not know as yet. But we will, my dears, we will!"

Twelve

A FEW DAYS later, Lady Catherine Cahill went with a party to Vauxhall. Lord Deeds had planned the evening, including boats to carry them there, when he learned Kitty had never seen the famous pleasure gardens. He had even arranged for a wind trio to accompany them in another boat, playing popular airs for his guests' amusement.

Mr. Kendall had not been included in the treat, but Kitty was not surprised. Lord Deeds had already taken her to task for favoring him so much, and Kitty had promised herself that sometime this evening, she would tell the earl that she would never marry him, and have done with it. He was much too possessive all of a sudden, as if their engagement was an accomplished fact, and she found she did not care for his attitude.

As they strolled the paths of Vauxhall a little later, before taking their seats in Lord Deed's box, she saw that Viscount Benning and Miss Gardner had also decided to attend the festivities with a group of friends, and her heart sank. Was she to see them everywhere she went? Was she never to be free of those dark blue eyes, that handsome face and strong, masculine body, a constant reminder of everything she had lost?

Kitty tried to enjoy the concert and the fireworks, and the antics of some of the lower-class people who were there in such bustling crowds. Her eyes widened when she noticed the number of demimondes about, eager to ply their trades, and the roving bands of young bloods just as anxious to accommodate them. She saw more than one transaction agreed on before the couple slipped away to a secluded spot. Kitty, herself, attracted a lot of attention with her fiery hair, and several coarse comments as well, and she stayed close to Lord Deeds's side.

But even though she found the evening eye-opening and unusual, she only toyed with the burnt ham shavings and little biscuits for which Vauxhall was famous. She did, however, have two glasses of champagne, for she was a little nervous about giving Lord Deeds his *congé*.

After supper, her host suggested they go for a further inspection of the gardens, and Kitty agreed as soon as she saw that the other guests were prepared to join them.

She never did find out why she was suddenly alone with the earl on a dark side path, but perhaps the champagne had made her careless. As he put his arms around her, she struggled.

"No, no, dear Kitty," he murmured as he stared down into her face. "It is time for another lesson in lovemaking, my dear. And the perfect place for it, too, for why should we not, as others are doing all around us, taste each other's delights?"

"I have decided I do not care to have any more lessons, m'lord," Kitty told him, but his arms only tightened at her waist. As she put her hands on his chest to push him away, he captured them in one of his hands.

"How coy you are!" he said, laughing at her a little. "But know I will not let you go this time until you agree to marry me, my love," he said.

Kitty was becoming alarmed. There was a dangerous glint in the earl's eyes, and she was aware he had a great deal more champagne than she had.

"I am sorry, but I have decided that we would not

suit, m'lord," she told him, feeling breathless. "Furthermore, my family has told me I would never be allowed to marry a man like you. I think it would be best if we did not see each other again."

The earl's face stiffened. "Is that so?" he asked, as if he did not care very much what she thought. "But you do not expect me to accept such an arrogant dismissal calmly, do you? Not after you have flirted with me, led me on? Oh, no, Kitty. Now you must pay the piper."

Suddenly he let her go and bowed to her. "Give you good evening, Lady Catherine Cahill," he said before he turned and walked away.

Kitty was startled, for she had expected she would have to fight off his advances. "Wait!" she cried. "Where are you going?"

The earl turned back, and the grim expression he wore on his aristocratic face, his narrowed eyes, made her gasp. "Why, I am going home, dear lady," he said calmly.

"But—but you cannot just *leave* me here!" Kitty exclaimed.

"I can't?" the earl asked. "But I will. It is no more than you deserve. You should have been more careful how you treated me, Lady Catherine, for now I find I do not care very much what happens to you." He smiled grimly then. "Although I am sure something *will* happen, before you reach home again, if you ever do," he added.

A short distance away, Kitty could hear some men laughing and making rude remarks about the women passing by, and she shivered. However was she to avoid being accosted? she wondered. Why, several times this evening, she knew she would have been approached by any number of men if she had not had the protection of the earl's arm. And now he was going to leave her to the mob's mercy! A mob that seemed to consider her horrid red hair an advertisement of her trade. How could he do such a thing?

"Yes, the young beaux will see to you, my dear," the earl told her in a flat, cold voice. "How satisfying it will be for me to contemplate! The lovely and admired Lady Catherine Cahill—the Incomparable of 1816—being dragged into the bushes and violated. And perhaps by more than one hot-blooded, dirty commoner. You may have scorned my lovemaking, my hand, but you will have a lesson this evening that you will never forget. You will be ruined, and I promise you I will make sure the news of your downfall becomes the latest *on dit.*"

He turned on his heels without another word, and walked swiftly away. For a moment, Kitty thought to run after him and beg him, as a gentleman, to reconsider, but then she stopped and squared her shoulders. She would not beg, not from the likes of him. He was in truth the devil the dowager had named him.

Another raucous shout of laughter came from the end of the walk, and she saw two men approaching. Quickly, she picked up her skirts and fled in the opposite direction. Behind her, she heard them calling "Yoicks!" and "Tallyho!" and the sounds of their boots as they thudded after her, and she tried to run faster. She could see many lanterns ahead, and she knew she would be safer on the main thoroughfare amid the large crowd. For even if someone harrassed her, they could not make her go with them, not with everyone watching. And perhaps she would be able to find an older couple to help her.

But she did not reach those bright lights that beckoned her to safely. Intead, she was seized from behind and spun around in a pair of burly arms. The man who had captured her was drunk, and his fetid breath washed over her and made her feel ill. As he grinned down at her, a gold tooth blinked in the light.

"Well, well, and wot 'ave we 'ere?" he asked, turning her chin to get a better view. He whistled then, and his arms tightened as he crowed, "Woi, our ship's come in, Dan, for 'ere's a pretty little bird! And a leddy, if I'm not mistook. Now, wot's a leddy like you doin' all alone, me pretty? It is too bad, but Alf'll see you're not lonesome no more, and Dan as well.''

He chuckled as he cupped her breasts. Kitty took a deep breath and screamed. At once, a big hand clamped over her mouth. Desperately, as his companion crowded around, laughing and pawing her, Kitty bit him as hard as she could.

He dropped his hand with a howl of pain, and as the man he had named Dan twisted her arm, Kitty screamed again. "Help! Oh, someone help me, please!"

For a moment, she was sure all was lost, but then a hard hand clamped down on her attacker's shoulder to pull him away from her and send him spinning to the ground in an untidy sprawl. Sobbing, Kitty backed away.

The man named Alf danced forward, his fists raised. But there was only a short scuffle before he was suddenly floored by a hard right. Both attackers lost any interest they might have had in continuing the fight then, and took to their heels. After all, there wasn't no sense in getting hurt, and that there gent had a deadly bunch of fives, they told each other as they ran. And there were plenty of other birds about to play with, after all, and no need for a mill, neither.

Kitty turned to thank her rescuer, and her green eyes widened when she saw Viscount Benning's fierce, angry glare. Miss Gardner hovered behind him, her own gentle face full of concern.

"Oh, Lion!" Kitty cried as she threw herself into his arms. "Oh, Lion!"

The viscount held her close against his chest, cradling her head with a reassuring hand. He wondered at the size of the lump he had in his throat as he did so, and why he was trembling almost as much as Kitty was.

"Let me take her, Lionel," Mary Gardner said. Reluctantly, the viscount gave her into his fiancée's care, and turned away to compose himself.

"It is all right now, my dear Lady Catherine," Miss Gardner said in her soft voice. "No one can harm you now, for Lionel will take care of you, and so will I."

Kitty nodded and bit her lip as the viscount came back to them.

"Lord Deeds was responsible for this? He left you here?" he asked, never taking his eyes from her face.

"Yes," Kitty told him. "I told him I would not marry him, and he was so angry he left me to make my own way home." She willed herself to stop shaking as she added, "He said I would be attacked, and it would serve me right."

"You may be sure I shall see that he pays for this insult with his life, Kitty," the viscount said, his voice deadly cold.

"No, no!" both ladies cried together, and then they exchanged startled glances.

"You must not do that, Lion. Besides, it was even my fault in a way. I—I did not refuse him very nicely. In fact, I insulted him," Kitty said, shaking her head. Then she added quickly, "But I want no revenge, and I could not bear it if you were in any danger."

As the two stared at each other, Mary Gardner had the strangest feeling that they had forgotten her completely.

"It would not do, Lionel," she made herself say. "It would only damage Lady Catherine's reputation, after all. Besides, no one knows of this but the three of us, and she was not harmed. All this is best forgotten as quickly as possible."

The two ladies watched anxiously as the viscount absorbed her sensible words. When he nodded at last, they sighed in unison.

"It shall be as you say, my prudent, discreet Mary," he told her. "But Kitty, even if I cannot take Lord Deeds to task, I am tempted to put *you* over my knee right here. Whatever were you thinking of to go apart with the man in a place like this, my girl? And after I warned you about him, too!''

''I did not realize how bad he was,'' Kitty replied, watching his angry face a little nervously. ''I never thought he would do such a terrible thing, truly, I did not. I—I guess I am very naive.''

''Lord Deeds shall receive a letter from me in the morning,'' the viscount said, his voice harsh and strained. ''He will not bother you again.''

''Surely that is not your place, Lionel,'' Mary Gardner pointed out, sounding a little reproving. ''Her father, or her brother, must take him to task. You are only a distant relation.''

As the viscount's cheekbones reddened and he nodded, she put her arm around Kitty's slender waist. ''Come, my dear Lady Catherine,'' she said. ''The viscount's carriage is nearby, and we will take you home. It grows late.''

It was a long time before Mary Gardner slept that night. After they had seen the Lady Catherine safely back to Berkeley Square and the viscount had taken her home as well, she had paced the floor of her bedchamber, deep in thought.

She had suspected for some time that Lionel Eden was in love with Lady Catherine Cahill, although she knew he was not aware of that love. No, she thought, shaking her head, the foolish man thinks it is only a family fondness he has for her, but I know differently.

And tonight, she had learned how deeply Lady Catherine loved him in return. It was there in her eyes, that shining light of love that she could not hide. And it was in her voice when she spoke to him, in all her gestures and posture. And to think she herself had never noticed before! Indeed, she had thought Lady Catherine much too young and careless, too wild and volatile to know true love. But she had been wrong.

She sighed as she climbed into bed at last, to lie sleepless, staring up at the dark ceiling. Whatever was she to do now? she wondered. For she could see her entire world and all her future crumbling around her, and she could not bear to contemplate such a disaster.

But she also knew she could not bear to contemplate any actions of hers that would keep them apart. Lionel was so wonderful, so dear to her, and he had done so much for her already. How could she even think of holding him, when he loved another?

Her eyes were heavy the next morning as she sipped her chocolate and made her plans. After she was dressed, she would send a note to Berkeley Square, and she would call on Lady Catherine this very day. It was the only honorable thing she could do, no matter how she shrank from it.

Kitty Cahill, who had gone to sleep at once, worn out from emotional exhaution, rose much earlier. She, too, wrote a note, but hers was directed to Lord Deeds. In it, she told him that no harm had come to her the previous evening, for she had been rescued by friends as soon as he had left her. And then she proceeded to tell him exactly what she thought of him, and suggested he leave London before she was tempted to tell her father or her brother about his treatment of her. It was an icy, cold note, and it gave her a great deal of satisfaction to seal it and send it on its way, carried by a running footman.

When she received Mary Gardner's request for an interview, she was tempted to claim she had a previous engagement. Of course, being so kind and good, Miss Gardner only wanted to make sure she was suffering no harm from her adventure. And perhaps she wishes to drop a few words of advice in my ear, Kitty told herself. She was older, after all, and wiser by far. But Kitty did not want to see her. She did not want to have to talk to the woman Lion loved. She knew it would be rude to refuse after all her help, however, so she agreed to receive her at three that afternoon.

She was glad when Katherine Elizabeth came by a

little later, for admiring the purchases her friend had made that morning at the Burlington Arcade allowed her to forget Lion's fiancée. And then Garth Allendon was announced as well.

He did not seem at all pleased to see Kitty's old crony sitting with her, but even though he wished Miss Rice would cut her visit short, he set himself to talking to both girls as any man of the world would.

But by some inexplicable circumstance he did not understand in the slightest, by the time Katherine Elizabeth did rise and announce her departure, he found himself offering to escort her home. Miss Rice smiled at him and blushed, her eyes lowered, and his chest swelled. How lovely she is, he thought to himself as she bade Lady Catherine good-bye. I wonder that I never noticed it before!

Why, with her bouncy curls and big blue eyes, her rosy cheeks and tempting curves, she was turning into a beauty! And she had seemed to admire him as well, look up to him as the sophisticate he was, in a way Lady Catherine never had. And if he had been honest, Garth Allendon would be the first to admit he was becoming very tired of proposing to a lady who only laughed at him, and refused him each and every time he asked for her hand.

Kitty chuckled as the door closed behind the pair, a most solicitous marquess carrying Katherine Elizabeth's packages and holding her arm as if she were some fragile thing in the greatest of danger. And she had to smile when she remembered her friend's artfulness this past half hour, all those blushing peeks at the young man, her obvious breathless admiration for his stories. And she was not even seventeen! Kitty could see that when she did make her comeout, Miss Rice would attract any number of beaux, for she had turned out to be a consummate flirt.

She was not smiling, however, when the butler announced Miss Mary Gardner later in the day. Kitty had arranged to meet the lady in one of the smaller salons. Her mother had gone out, but there was no telling when she would return. And Kitty had no desire for her mama to learn a single thing about what had happened to her at Vauxhall. No, indeed!

She wondered at how pale and tired looking Mary Gardner looked as she took her seat and thanked her hostess for receiving her. And she was puzzled when that lady turned to make sure the butler had closed the door tightly behind him when he left the room.

Only then did she lean closer, and, lowering her voice, say, "You must forgive me for asking such a personal question, Lady Catherine, but are you, as I suspect, in love with Lionel Eden?"

Kitty started, one hand going to her throat. For a moment, she was tempted to deny it, for she did not think she could bear for Mary Gardner to learn of her love. As she hesitated, her visitor said earnestly, "You must believe me when I tell you my question is important, or I would never ask such a thing."

Kitty stared into her serious face, those intent dark eyes, and she nodded. This was not just idle curiosity at work. "Yes, I am," she admitted. "I have loved him since I was twelve years old. I begged him to wait for me to grow up, but, as you are well aware, he did not."

"I see you are a steadfast girl, indeed," Miss Gardner said. "I am just such a one myself."

Kitty felt her face stiffening, for she was sure she was about to be chastised, told she could never have Lion, that Miss Gardner would never let him go. And she already knew that.

"Do not look so, Lady Catherine," Mary Gardner said instead as she patted her hand. "I have a story to tell you, and when I am done, you will understand. But I must have your promise that not a single word I am about to say will ever be revealed by you to a living soul. Do I have that promise?"

Mystified, Kitty agreed, and her guest settled back in her chair with a sigh.

"My story begins many years ago," Miss Gardner started. "My home is near Falmouth, and when I was seventeen, just your age, m'lady, I fell in love with a young man in the neighborhood. His name is Alexander Wadley. Our families did not move in the same circles, however. You see, my father had been a rich man, with extensive estates and august connections, and Alex was only the orphaned son of an ordinary seaman. He lived with his grandmother in the town."

She sighed again, and smiled to herself, and Kitty took a deep breath, suddenly realizing she had quite forgotten to do so for some time.

"Alex fell in love with me, too," Mary Gardner continued. "We did not see each other often, for he had joined the Royal Navy, following in his father's footsteps. First as a cabin boy, then as a gunner. But when he gained the rank of lieutenant, as a reward for unusual bravery in action, he dared to ask my mother for my hand. She would not even consider it. She was a proud woman, born of the peerage, and since I was an only child, and my father's sole heir, she intended me to marry as high as she could arrange it.

"I begged, I pleaded with her, but she would not listen. And so I had to tell Alex in the few minutes that she allowed me to see him alone to say good-bye, that all I could do was wait for him, and pray I could get my mother to change her mind. I told him I would never marry until that someday when we could be together. He said he would wait for me, too. Till eternity, he said."

Miss Gardner looked down at her clasped hands. "Eventually, my mother wearied of taking me to London and introducing me to those gentlemen she considered to be worthy of my hand, for I refused each and every one. And then, after receiving a letter from my uncle, she decided we should go on a visit to the West Indies. I think she imagined that Uncle George, being a man, would be able to influence me more than she could herself. Little did she suspect what awaited us in Jamaica!''

Suddenly, Miss Gardner raised her handkerchief to her face, and Kitty heard her stifle a sob. She was so spellbound by the story she was hearing, she could not even speak a word of sympathy.

"You see, my Uncle George coveted my inheritance," Mary Gardner went on after a moment to compose herself. "Oh, it is not that he is not well-do-do himself, but he is one of those men who must always have more. His life is ruled by his greed for gold. And he decided that the way to get my money was to marry me to my cousin Franklin.''

"Surely not Franklin Dedham?" Kitty asked in a horrified voice.

"The very same," Miss Gardner told her. "You can imagine my revulsion at that possibility. But Franklin, besides being half-witted and completely under my uncle's thumb, was delighted at the thought of marriage to me, and he made my life a misery. But enough of that.''

Mary Gardner shuddered before she went on, "I begged my mother to stand firm, not to listen to my uncle's reasoned arguments for keeping the money in the family. And then she fell ill from the fever. I could see that she was sinking fast, and I knew when she was gone, my uncle would force me to marry Franklin. He had already told me he would starve and beat me until I agreed, and that if I continued rebellious, he would arrange an accidental death for me. That way he would inherit directly.''

Kitty gasped, and Miss Gardner nodded, her eyes bleak with her memories.

"I went out for a walk one afternoon, for he would not allow me to use the carriage or a riding horse lest I try to escape," she went on. "And as I was sitting and resting, and crying in despair, Viscount Benning came along. We knew each other slightly, of course, from various parties we had both attended since my arrival.

"He insisted I tell him what was troubling me, and when I did so under his kind prompting and concern, he became determined to save me. He wanted to take me to his aunt, but I knew I could not stay at Golden Grove. Uncle George would have come after me, and insisted, as was his right, that I return to my family. He is my guardian, after my mother, you see.

"So then the viscount came up with another plan. He said we would pretend to be engaged, and he would bring me back to England and to Alex. That way I would be safe until I was reunited with him. He said it was the only way, and I—I agreed."

She looked up at Kitty then, and something in her face made her add quickly, "Do not quite hate me, my dear, please! I had no other choice, none at all!"

Kitty shook her head and tried to smile, and Mary Gardner went on, "Fortunately, I was able to gain my mother's consent that same afternoon. Lionel was noble, after all, and she had never liked the thought of any union with Franklin Dedham. And after she died, and we buried her, Lionel made plans for us to take ship for home."

Miss Gardner coughed a little then, and Kitty was quick to go and pour her a glass of water. She thanked her and sipped for a moment before she said, "We never dreamed my uncle would insist on coming back with us, to watch us. We never thought the engagement would ever have to be announced in England at all. But Uncle George was furious at losing my money, and he seemed to have suspicions about our sudden attachment. You do see why we had to announce the engagement, for Alex is at sea, and no one knows when he will return to England. Last fall we had word that his ship had called at Gibraltar before sailing to India. I do not know where he is now, and neither does Lionel, although he haunts the Admiralty for news.

"And I am sure you can see why it is of primary importance that Uncle George never learn a word of my deceit. I think he would kill me if he knew, for I suspect the madness that afflicts Franklin Dedham has roots in his brain as well."

"How ghastly for you, Miss Gardner!" Kitty cried, unable to keep silent another moment. "You may be sure I shall never say a word!"

Mary Gardner smiled a little. "I do not wonder that you love Lionel Eden, Lady Catherine. He is so good, so caring a man! I will always be grateful to him for his help, and his insistence that we continue the farce for my protection. He had no thought of himself at all."

"But why didn't he tell *me*?" Kitty asked, frowning now. "He must have known I could be trusted to keep the secret, and yet he has let me go all this time in the most awful misery and dejection. I cannot believe he could be so cruel!"

Mary Gardner patted her hand again. "He did not believe in your love, my dear. He thought it was only a girlish fancy that you would outgrow. And even now, he does not suspect how much he himself loves you. He thinks he is only fond of you, as he has always been fond of his little Miss Kittycat."

"He—he *does* love me? How do you know?" Kitty asked, her green eyes beginning to glow with hope.

Miss Gardner admired them as she nodded. "Oh, yes, I have known of it for some time, and that is why I told you my story. The way Lionel has watched you—his constant preoccupation with whom you were with, what you were doing—his fury at Lord Deeds last evening—if those are not the actions of a man in love, I do not know what are!"

Kitty clasped her hands tightly together to hide their trembling. "I do so pray you are right, Miss Gardner," she said.

"Please call me Mary, my dear," her guest requested. "For after all, we share a secret now. And I would remind you of your promise. You must not tell a soul, not even the viscount, that you know my story. For if you were to do so, he might reveal his love for you, and then my uncle would find out. I know it is hard, and I wish I did not have to ask it of you, but can you wait? Just until my dear Alex returns?"

Kitty put back her head and laughed. "Wait for Lion?" she asked. "I, like your gallant officer, would wait an eternity! And after all, I have waited five long years for him. What is another month—or even six?"

The two sat on in the small salon for some time, telling each other of their different loves, and comparing their circumstances. It seemed to ease Mary Gardner's mind to be able to speak openly, let her guard down at last. Perhaps she had been longing for a friend in order to do so, Kitty thought. What a burden she had carried alone all this time!

So when the lady finally rose to leave, Kitty came and kissed her cheek and hugged her, and the eyes of both of them were wet as she did so.

Quite unusually, Lady Catherine Cahill had no engagements for that evening, and she was delighted. She excused herself soon after the tea tray had been brought in, telling her parents that she was very tired.

Lady Deane excused her gladly. She knew Kitty had been overdoing, but even so, as she told her husband, she did not think she had ever seen her looking better. "Why, there is a positive bloom about her all of a sudden," she said.

Lord Deane agreed as he sipped his tea. "Perhaps she is forgetting the viscount at last?" he suggested.

"How grand if that were so!" Rose Cahill said fervently. "For although I should not say it, and I know it was not his fault that Kitty fell in love with him, sometimes I wish Lionel Eden had never been born!"

Upstairs, Lady Catherine settled down in her big postered bed to dream of the man her parents were castigating so fervently in the drawing room below her.

But before she did so, she prayed that His Majesty's frigate *Resolute,* commanded by the newly appointed Captain Alexander Wadley, was even then making for a home port at last.

Thirteen

KITTY WOKE EARLY the next morning, and although her first thought was of Lion as always, she wondered why she felt so uneasy and dejected. It was a puzzle, for she had fallen asleep last night with a delighted smile on her lips.

Later, as she sipped her chocolate and stared out at the misty rain that was falling, she realized that she had been spinning dreams again, dreams that might never come true. For even though Lion was not really engaged, she had only Mary Gardner's word for it that he loved her. And Mary might be mistaken.

And she herself did not think she could bear to be disappointed again. No, she must not build any castles in the air, not yet. She must watch and wait and pray.

But, oh, it was so very hard when she longed to go to Lion and speak to him! How she wanted to tell him that she knew everything, and revered him for his chivalry. And most of all, try and discover if what Mary had told her was true.

But she could not do that. She had given her promise. And she could see how dangerous it would be for Mary Gardner if she did not keep that promise. She cast her mind back to the story she had heard yesterday. She had not thought there was such wickedness in the world! What a terrible man George Gardner was, and what an awful life Mary had had to live. When she compared it to her own, she was humbled, for she was surrounded by a loving family, a father and mother who adored her, a brother and sister who cared for her, and the dowager duchess who was such a good friend! But Mary had known only her father's early death, her mother's unyielding pride, and a wicked uncle bent on gaining her fortune while she was separated from the man she loved.

Kitty saw that she must do everything she could to help her. And since the only way she could help at the moment was to remain silent, that was the course she would have to follow.

She decided that she must try and avoid Lion, for she was not at all sure she would not give the game away if she were close to him.

And so, for the first time that Season, Lady Catherine Cahill began to refuse invitations to any affair where the handsome viscount and his supposed fiancée might appear. Her mother wondered at it, but she was a little relieved that Kitty was abating the furious pace she had set at the beginning of the Season.

The dowager duchess wondered at it as well, but neither lady was able to get her to discuss it. Kitty only claimed she was tired and a little bored; that she had come to see that one party looked forward to with anticipation, was much more satisfying than so many she could not even remember them at all.

Lionel Eden noticed that Kitty was less in company than before, and he asked Mary Gardner if she had any idea why. They were attending a reception that evening, and the viscount had been sure Kitty Cahill would be there. And when she did not come, he was perturbed. He noticed Mary glancing around as if she were afraid she might be overheard, and he remembered that Mr. Gardner had also been invited to attend this evening's party.

"I am sure she is all right, Lionel," she said softly.

"But perhaps something did happen to her that night

at Vauxhall," the viscount persisted. "Perhaps she was so frightened, so upset, it preys on her mind even now."

Miss Gardner smiled and pressed his hand. "Courageous Kitty Cahill?" she asked with a chuckle. "She is not afraid of anything, and you know it!"

The viscount grinned a little as he nodded.

"Besides, Lord Deeds has gone to the country," Mary continued. "And I do not believe I told you, but I called on Lady Catherine the day after we were all at Vauxhall. I had to be sure she was all right, and so I can tell you she was none the worse for her adventure."

Lionel Eden looked at her fondly. "You are too good, Mary," he said, raising her hand to his lips to kiss.

Across the room, Miss Hetty Dedham tittered and poked George Gardner, nodding her head in the direction of the young lovers. Mr. Gardner snorted and looked more unpleasant than ever.

Of course, there were those occasions that both Kitty and the viscount attended even so. And the viscount noticed at once how quiet she had become. Gone was the laughing flirt who had captivated the gentlemen earlier, even though she was still popular, and Paul Kendall was often by her side. Lionel Eden frowned when he saw how persistent the man was. He was sure he was bent on attaching Kitty, for he did not appear to be at all discouraged by her sudden lack of enthusiasm for his company. Then Lord Benning wondered why he felt so depressed. He knew Paul Kendall was a good man, and if anyone could be said to be worthy of Kitty Cahill, he was that man. But although he knew he should be happy for her, and pleased, perversely he found the situation most distasteful. He did not understand himself at all.

But even though Kitty was often in his thoughts, he forgot her the day he learned that the frigate *Resolute* had anchored at Plymouth at last, and that her captain was on his way to London to make his report to the

Admiralty. Lord Benning hurried to the Dedham townhouse, and when he heard Mr. Gardner's testy voice coming from the library where he was chastising his nephew for some misdeed, he invited Mary to come for a walk with him. He did not dare take the risk of telling her the good news anywhere in her uncle's vicinity.

He was glad he had been so cautious when he saw her reaction. For a moment, she swayed, her eyes closed and her face so ashen he put his arm around her at once in support. "Are you all right, my dear?" he asked, his voice serious.

She nodded, biting her lip. And then she looked up at him, and he caught his breath at the happiness he saw shining in her brown eyes. "Oh, yes, I am! At last I am," she whispered. "How long will it be before I can see him, Lionel?" she asked.

"I have left a message for him at the Admiralty," the viscount told her. "As soon as he gets in touch with me, we will make plans for your reunion. And I'm sure it won't be long now, my dear Mary, until you are happy again!"

"And you as well, my dear sir," she told him. But when he questioned her, she only smiled and shook her head.

Captain Wadley appeared on Lord Benning's doorstep two days later. The viscount liked him at once. He was a man of above medium height, with neat blond hair and eyes the color of many of the stormy oceans he had sailed for so many years. There was an air of quiet strength and calm assurance about him as well, and although he was a little stiff when he first learned about the viscount's engagement to Miss Mary Gardner, he was soon smiling and shaking Lionel Eden's hand with fervor.

The two men spent an hour together, discussing Mary and the entire situation that had led to their deception. The captain would have liked to challenge Mr. George

Gardner for his brutal treatment of his niece, but the viscount managed to dissuade him.

"I do assure you, captain," Lord Benning said earnestly, eyeing the man's stern expression and suddenly compressed mouth, "Mr. Gardner has been punished enough. He has lost Mary's wealth, and he has been forced to remain in England all this time. Mary is twenty-seven now, and I doubt any court would agree even if he were so foolhardy as to try to have your marriage annulled, once it is a *fait accompli.*"

He watched the other man a little nervously, until Captain Wadley nodded in reluctant agreement. The viscount, seeing his still angry eyes and the white lines that bracketed his mouth, was very glad he had never served under the man and incurred his displeasure in any way.

After the captain took his leave, with many fervent words of gratitude, the viscount wrote a note to Mary, asking her to join him for a drive in the park the following morning at ten. It was not the usual time of day for such excursions, but perhaps it would not cause any speculation among her relations, since they were engaged. And he knew Mary would be able to interpret his invitation correctly, for she was as aware as Lionel Eden of the desperate need for subterfuge.

The viscount chose his closed carriage for the drive. As he helped Mary Gardner up the steps of it, he saw how disappointed she was that it was empty, and he squeezed her hand. He knew she had expected to see her gallant captain there, waiting for her. When the viscount explained that he considered that too dangerous so close to home, she agreed at once. By previous arrangement, the carriage stopped briefly at the Stanhope Gate, and Captain Wadley joined them there, taking the seat beside the woman he had loved for such a very long time.

Lionel Eden had wanted to see for himself that the

love his gentle Mary had for this man truly was returned, for he had come to love her himself, as he would his sister. But when he saw the captain's stern face relax in a smile of joy, the way he took her in his arms so tenderly and kissed her, all his doubts disappeared. He banged on the roof then, and ordered the carriage to halt. The two lovers looked at him, a little confused, and Mary blushed as he excused himself.

"I am most definitely *de trop* here," he told her with a twinkle in his eye. "And you will want to be alone to make your plans. I shall order the coachman to drive out into the country, and return for me here in an hour."

Captain Wadley's handshake was eloquent, but when he would have voiced his thanks again, the viscount only waved them away.

When he rejoined them, he found Mary held so tightly in Captain Wadley's arms, it was as if he could not bear to let her go. He noticed that she was smiling with her happiness, and her eyes were like two stars. Alexander Wadley also wore a triumphant grin. Lionel Eden wondered at the pang he felt at their jubilation, but he forced himself to disregard it, as they all discussed the coming wedding.

The captain took charge of the conversation. It was obvious it had become a habit since he was so used to command, aboard his ship. Lionel Eden sat back, content to listen as Wadley discussed the special license he meant to obtain so an immediate ceremony could take place.

"Mary had convinced me that we must make haste, lest her uncle discover the *Resolute* is in harbor and her captain in town," he said, and then he turned and smiled down at the woman by his side and added more softly, "Not that I am at all reluctant to have it so. I have waited too many years already for my bride, and now I find I have no desire to wait a moment longer than is necessary to get all in train. We will leave

London for Plymouth immediately after the ceremony, and we should be miles away before Gardner discovers anything is amiss."

The viscount agreed that this was an excellent plan. But when they dropped the captain off and the carriage headed back to the Dedham townhouse, he asked Mary if she would mind marrying without her bride clothes, and not even able to bring a portmanteau with her. She laughed at him.

"How unimportant all that is, Lionel," she said. "Just to have Alex close to me again, to be able to look forward to our life together, is more than enough for me. And it would be more than enough for Lady Catherine Cahill, too," she added.

At the viscount's arrested expression, she said, "My dear Lionel! Yes, I know she loves you, and I suspect she always will. I was not sure until that night at Vauxhall, for I will confess I had not thought her capable of such devotion before then. She seemed much too young and careless—too flighty and flirtatious. But I came to see that that was just a pose she assumed, thinking you were lost to her forever. But the way she threw herself into your arms, the love in her eyes, and her voice when she cried out your name made it only too clear to me that you were as dear to her as Alex is to me."

She smiled at him then, and added, "And I know something else, my dear friend. You love her in return. I have known it this age, and I have prayed that some day you would be able to speak of it to her, when you are free of the burden I have been to you."

She saw the viscount was about to speak, and she shook her head at him. "Look deep into your heart, sir, and see if what I am telling you is not true. For why else have you been so concerned for her? Why else did you consider every man who even smiled at her to be unworthy of her? Have you any idea how your eyes follow her, how you watch her so closely every chance you get? And have you never stopped to wonder why it makes you so happy to talk about her to me? Dear Lionel! What you thought was a family fondness is no such thing. But you will see, and soon, that I am right!"

It was a disquieting time for the viscount and Mary Gardner until the captain obtained the special license and made the wedding arrangements. Lionel Eden was careful to behave just as he had been doing all these past months. He escorted Mary to a reception and the theater, took tea with her and Miss Hetty Dedham, and he drove her in his phaeton in Hyde Park every fine afternoon.

Sometimes he wondered that she could be so calm, so easy, and he watched her with a little awe as she went through these tense days in her usual well-bred manner.

He saw Kitty Cahill only once, and then at a distance. She was riding in the park with Paul Kendall, and they had stopped to greet some friends. As the viscount admired her slim figure in its emerald green habit, the brilliance of the curls peeping out beneath the brim of her riding bonnet, he was reminded how Mary had assured him of her love. For some reason, he found it dangerous to consider that now. No, until Mary was safe, he would try and put Kitty from his mind. Time enough to ponder what Mary had told him after the ceremony.

That event took place in a small church on the outskirts of London on a beautiful morning in June. Viscount Benning was the captain's groomsman, and the vicar's wife was pressed into service as bridesmaid and witness. And before the happy couple drove away, the new Mrs. Wadley took Lionel Eden's face between her hands and drew it down so she could give him a heartfelt kiss.

"I can never thank you enough for all you have done for me, Lionel," she said. "And I pray you will find your own happiness soon. It is much closer than you think, my dear. But I beg you will have a care for my uncle. He is not completely sane, you know. And when he discovers how he has been hoodwinked, he may well try and do you some harm."

Mary had told her uncle that the viscount was taking her down to Benning for the day, and that they would not return to town until late in the afternoon, for she wanted to be sure she and her new husband were far away when he discovered the hoax. And although she had worried that he might insist on accompanying them, or sending Franklin Dedham in his stead, fortune smiled on her at last. Both gentlemen were involved with business at their bank on her wedding day, so she was able to escape the house without hindrance. But still, she could not help but feel guilty at the danger Lionel Eden might be in.

She looked so worried, the viscount smiled broadly to reassure her. "Surely you refine on it too much, Mary," he said. "He would not dare! Now, be off on your bride trip, and forget him and all the unhappiness he has caused you both."

Captain Wadley shook the viscount's hand, and Lionel Eden was glad he was so overcome with his emotion that he was unable to say a single word. He felt he had been thanked overmuch as it was.

He went home with a light heart. He knew Mary had left a note for her uncle, telling him of her marriage and pretending that he himself had not been aware of it, or of her deception all this time. He was sure that was enough to guarantee his safety, no matter how furious the man was. But still, knowing the storm of gossip that would begin when news of the broken engagement and the sudden marriage to another man, became known, he decided to go to Benning.

Besides, he needed time to think. Think hard. Mary had been so sure that Kitty still loved him, but he could not believe it, not after the way he had treated her. And not when he remembered how she had flirted and smiled and danced her way through the Season, as if she had never been in love at all. And he admitted that he himself was confused about the way he felt for her. Mary's words echoed in his mind now. He must have been obvious in his concern for Kitty, if Mary had seen it so clearly. But did that concern mean love? Or was it only the result of his fondness for his Miss Kittycat? No, he decided, it was best to go away and sort out his thoughts before he saw her again.

As he was making the arrangments to do so, Kitty Cahill was reading the long letter Mary Gardner had sent to her that morning. In it, she told her of her wedding, and thanked her for all her understanding and her reticence. At the end, she mentioned how worried she was that her uncle might try to do the viscount some harm. Kitty, who had smiled at the beginning of the letter, frowned now. Yes, she thought as she began to pace the room, Mary was right. In his fury at being deceived, Mr. Gardner might well strike out at the man who had aided his niece, and helped her to defy him. But what could she do to ensure Lion's safety? she wondered. Clearly it was up to her to protect him, since she was the only one who knew the whole story. She wished she might talk to the dowager duchess and beg her assistance, for she could see she was on dangerous ground. But there was still her promise to Mary not to tell a single soul. No, this was something she must do alone, and do well, even as unexperienced in intrigue as she was.

It was some time later before her worried frown disappeared, and she hurried to her writing desk. She would send the infamous Mr. George Gardner an anonymous letter, telling him she knew everything— how he had threatened his niece to force her into marriage with his simpleminded heir, and his plans to murder her if she would not agree. And she would warn him that if anything happened to Lionel Eden, Viscount Benning, while he and his nephew remained in England, she would be quick to inform the authorities, and have him taken up for murder.

After the letter was written, she read it over, and then she added a postscript to the effect that the sooner he returned to Jamaica, the better it would be for him.

Fourteen

THE GOSSIP THAT swept through the *ton,* like the fires that had swept through the narrow attached tenements of London on so many sad occasions, was just as violent as the viscount had foreseen. The polite world was amazed and titillated, and for several days the duped Viscount Benning and the treacherous Miss Mary Gardner were the only subjects discussed in every gentleman's club and at every lady's tea party.

Lady Deane and her daughter received an urgent summons from the Dowager Duchess of Wynne, asking them to call at once, as soon as she heard the news. Rose Cahill was delighted to do so. She had been stunned and dismayed that Lionel Eden had been so deceived, and astounded at how calmly Kitty was taking the news.

As soon as they had taken their seats in the dowager's drawing room, that good lady told them what she had learned from Jane and Eliza's visits to the Dedham home. "But never would I have expected such devious behavior from such a genteel, quiet young woman," she concluded, sounding miffed that she had been so deceived by Miss Gardner. "And to think she managed to delude Lionel all these months! She is a consummate actress, and no better than a Jezebel! It is too bad!"

When neither of her visitors had a comment, she went on, "And she has known this Captain Wadley for a long time. It is not as if she accepted Lionel's suit in good faith and then found she had mistaken her heart. I cannot believe such infamy!''

The dowager shook her head so violently that several hairpins went flying. And then, catching sight of Kitty's serene smile, she was dumbfounded. "It appears that you know a great deal more about this than either your mama or I do, puss," she said tartly. "I wonder you did not tell us long before this."

"I couldn't," Kitty admitted "I cannot tell you even now, although I do assure you, Mary Gardner is no Jezebel. But she swore me to secrecy, so you do see you must not press me, ma'am."

The dowager sniffed. "Very well. I would never ask you to betray a confidence. But now we must put our heads together and see what we can do for Lionel to bring him out of this with a whole skin. I would not have him or anyone in the family laughed at and maligned."

"Emery told me he has gone down to Benning," Rose Cahill volunteered. "Perhaps if he is not seen in town for some time, the gossip will die down. Then, too, the Season is almost over. Perhaps by the time the *ton* assembles in force again, the whole thing will have been forgotten."

Kitty thought her mama sounded very dubious about such a miracle's ever taking place.

"Yes, that might happen," the dowager said slowly. "But from long experience, I think more direct action is called for. It is such a magnificent scandal!"

She frowned, and both Cahill ladies waited quietly, knowing she was deep in thought.

At last she sighed and said, "I do believe I will begin to set it about that Lionel knew Mary Gardner loved the captain, and because of her uncle's refusal to condone the match, he offered himself as a decoy to lead him off the scent until their marriage could take place. I, myself, would laugh if told such a fairy tale, asked to believe such selfless chivalry, but perhaps if we spout it often and loudly enough, it will come to be believed. Rose, you must do your share to bruit it about, too.''

Kitty was startled to see how close her old friend had come to the truth, but she did not say anything. The dowager had already told them that Mr. Gardner and his nephew were making plans to sail home to Jamaica the first of next week, so she knew her letter had done the trick, and now she could be easy for Lion. And what was a little gossip, after all?

But still, she felt as if she were standing on tiptoe, waiting breathlessly for what would happen next. It was impossible for her to go down to Benning, no matter how she longed to do so, and she knew it. There was nothing she could do but wait, as she had promised herself she would. As in any chess match, it was clearly the viscount's move.

So in the days that followed, when her mother began to talk about removing to Deane for the summer months, she begged her to delay. She did not feel she could bear to leave town without seeing him.

Yet when she considered talking her dilemma over with the dowager duchess, she was, for the first time, loathe to do so. No, she knew there must be no more manipulating on her part, no timely assistance from her old friend. This was between Lion and herself, and it was his turn to seek her out if he chose to do so. And if what Mary had told her was true, then he would seek her out. She would wait for that day, no matter how impatiently, telling herself that impulsive little Kitty Cahill was no more. And it was important that she do so, for she did not want Lion to propose to her because he felt guilty at the pain she had suffered at his hands. No, indeed. She wanted him to propose because he loved her to distraction, the same way she loved him.

She wondered that she could be so calm, so reasonable, when all her future was at stake.

At Benning, Lionel Eden tried to busy himself with estate matters, but since the crops had been planted, and everything was running smoothly under his new agent's capable direction, there was very little for m'lord to do. He found himself sitting and thinking, more often than not, for although a few old friends rode out to see him, to give him their assurances of esteem and support, for the most part he was alone.

He had only dared ask Emery Cahill, one of his first callers, for general news of the family. And that was unfortunate, for he had come to see how much he missed Kitty Cahill, how he longed especially for news of her. All these past months, when she had been cutting a dash through the *ton,* at least he had been able to watch her, and admire her. Now, it was as if she were very far away, and completely unattainable. And late one night, standing at his library windows, he realized that it was more than just missing her. He loved her as deeply as Mary had claimed he did.

How could I have been so blind? he asked himself as her wide green eyes and fiery curls came to his mind and he pictured her graceful, slender body; remembered her courage, passion, and wit. And he was humbled when he considered how long she had been true to him, how deep her love for him was. He remembered how she had kissed him and declared her love for him on the steps of Wynne when she was only twelve, how she had made him see what Benning could be under his own careful care, even how she had ridden out to denounce him and declare her love again, after she heard of his betrothal. Surely he was not worthy of such a faithful "Lady Lochinvar!"

And then he wondered if she loved him still, as Mary claimed she did. Had her gaiety this Season been only an act after all? He found himself praying that it was so.

But even if she did still love him, and he was free to marry her now, he did not see how Lord Deane could welcome him as a suitor. What? His daughter to be courted by the man all London was laughing at? No, no, he would never permit such a thing! Why, Lady

Catherine Cahill could have anyone she chose, from Garth Allendon to the impressive Mr. Paul Kendall. Why would the Cahills allow her to settle for such a shabby object of fun as he had become? For he knew well the gossip about him, the sly ridicule, and the cruel cartoons would go on and on, never to be forgotten completely. And would Kitty herself want him now? Perhaps his misadventure with Mary Gardner and all its dire consequences had changed her mind about him at last.

Lionel Eden groaned, and tried to forget her, for he knew it was the most honorable thing he could do.

But not many days later, he realized that even if he were repulsed by both Kitty and her family, he had to try. He loved her too dearly—wanted her too much—not to.

He decided he would go to London and call on the dowager duchess first. She was a wise woman, and one he trusted. Perhaps she could help him, tell him what he must do to win Kitty, he thought. Perhaps she could even give him the words he would need to persuade Kitty that this newfound love of his was real.

He ordered a horse brought around very early the next morning, and went to bed happier than he had been for some time.

Viscount Benning arrived in Berkeley Square at exactly ten o'clock, surprising the dowager, who was still at the breakfast table.

She told him to help himself to food and coffee, and, as he did so, she had a quiet word with her butler before she dismissed him.

After the servant bowed and left the room, she said, "How glad I am that you have come, dear boy! Indeed, although I should be angry with you for tearing off to Benning with nary a word of explanation to me, I am so delighted to see you, I shall not scold you."

"I—I have come to ask your help, ma'am," her guest said.

The dowager noticed the viscount was only toying with his eggs, scones, and finnan haddie, and her lips quirked. He was paler, too, and there was a bewildered frown in his dark blue eyes.

"But of course. I shall be pleased to do anything I can," she assured him.

"I hope your assistance will serve," Lord Benning muttered, running a hand through his auburn hair. "I confess I have no idea how to go about it, though I have searched my mind for hours. And it is so important to me, too, the most important thing of my life. . . ."

"Go about what, man?" the dowager asked bluntly, cutting through his confusing verbiage to get to the heart of the matter.

"Asking Kitty Cahill to marry me," he blurted out, and then he frowned. "You see, I have discovered I love her, that I have loved her for months, perhaps even for years, but I was too stupid to realize it."

"Do not worry about that, my dear boy," the dowager told him kindly. "Most men are just as stupid as you have been when it comes to the state of their hearts."

The viscount ignored this disparagement of his sex to lean forward and say, "But don't you see? After the affair with Mary—although I had a very good reason for it, you may be sure, ma'am—why would Kitty's father even entertain the thought of such a fool for his daughter? What, Lady Catherine Cahill marry a laughingstock? If I were Lord Deane, I'd show such a poor speciman the door at once, and cut the connection, even if we are family."

"It seems to me it is more important that Kitty can still stomach you," the dowager told him bluntly. "She has always been able to wrap her father around her little finger. So if she still wants you, you may be sure Reginald Cahill, and his wife as well, will be delighted to agree to it."

"But there is still that business with Mary," he said.

"Will Kitty understand that? Accept it? I cannot tell anyone the whole of it even now."

"I believe she knows something about that already," the dowager told him, and then she sniffed and added, "Miss Gardner spoke to her some time ago, but swore her to secrecy. Why, even *I* have no idea what it is all about!"

Lionel Eden stared at her, ignoring her slightly injured air as hope dawned in his eyes. "Pray I can convince Kitty of my love even so, ma'am," he said. "If only I did not feel so awkward, so—so unmanned! I am like a schoolboy writhing with his first infatuation. On the one hand, dying to confess it, yet, on the other, somehow shy and fearful of rejection." He groaned. "At this rate, I am sure to make a terrible botch of it!"

The dowager snorted and got to her feet. "Since you are doing nothing but pushing that good food around on your plate, Lionel, I think it is safe to say you have concluded breakfast."

The viscount rose and walked with her to the door.

"Just wait for me in the drawing room, if you would be so good, dear boy," his hostess said. "I have a most important note to write, but when that has been accomplished, I shall rejoin you and we will put our heads together on your problem. Somehow, I do not think it is the insurmountable dilemma you suppose."

Lionel Eden thanked her, and she went away. He, himself, walked slowly to the drawing room, deep in thought. Perhaps he should go over to the Deane town house this very morning, and put his courage to the sticking point before he lost his nerve, he told himself as he let himself into the room and closed the doors behind him.

And then he stood very still just inside those doors and stared, as his heart behaved in a most alarming way. For Lady Catherine Cahill was curled up in a large wing chair near one of the windows, looking through a set of fashion plates. She was dressed in a pretty pale blue

morning gown, and her plumed hat and gloves rested on
a table by her side.

The sunlight streaming into the room turned her curls
to golden fire, such a contrast to the creamy pearl of her
skin. As he watched her, standing perfectly still and
holding his breath in wonder and yearning, she looked
up, and her green eyes widened.

Speechless, the viscount held out his hand to her.
"Kitty?" he managed to say, cursing himself for his
lack of eloquence.

For a moment, he was sure she was lost to him, for
she sat as still as any statue, one slim hand at her throat.

Aching with his love for her, Lionel Eden held out his
arms, his face imploring. "Kitty, my dear love?" he
asked again. "Is it too late for me?"

In one quick flash of motion, she was on her feet to
run into his arms. As they closed around her in a fierce
embrace that left her breathless, she closed her eyes and
smiled.

"Oh, my darling Kitty," he whispered against her
curls. "What a terrible fool I have been! I have
discovered that I love you so much it hurts, and every
moment I am not with you brings me pain. Tell me I
have not come to my senses too late, that you love me
still!"

Kitty looked up at him, her heart in her eyes, and he
caught his breath in wonder at the emotion he saw
glowing there.

"How silly you are, dear Lion," she chided him. "Of
course I love you. I will love you all my life. . . ."

His heart suddenly felt much too big for his chest,
and Lionel Eden bent his head and kissed her as he had
been longing to do. The sweet scent he remembered
enveloped him, and as she put her arms around him and
surrendered her lips to his kiss, he felt once more the
wild exultation he had experienced at Deane and at
Vauxhall when he had had her in his arms.

It was a long time before he could bear to end that kiss. As they drew a little apart, Kitty smiled and reached up to touch the auburn locks that had fallen over his broad forehead. Her eyes never left his as she did so. And when she saw the light that was glowing in his dark blue eyes, she thought she must die for happiness.

"Know I will love you all my life, too, my faithful Lady Lochinvar," he told her, his voice a little unsteady. As her hand moved to caress the strong planes of his face, he added, "My darling, darling girl! And although you have not asked it of me, I can explain all about Mary Gardner. I know she would not mind if I told you. . . ."

She put her hand gently over his mouth, and he kissed it, his eyes closed with the emotion he was feeling. "I already know, Lion," she said. "Mary came to me and told me everything. How wonderful you were to help her, stand by her! I revere you for what you did for her, truly I do."

"Even though the *ton* think me a fool?" he asked, frowning a little now.

"Oh, the *ton*! Who cares what *they* think?" she asked airily, for all the world as if she had not just spent the last two months intent on captivating society.

"And your father—your mother?" he asked. "How will they like giving their daughter to a cuckold? Oh Kitty, I am so sorry bring this trouble to you!"

He saw she was shaking her head, and he stopped, somewhat amazed.

"But with all that the dowager has been telling the *ton,* if we are married in a short time, everyone will know you were not duped at all," she pointed out in a reasonable voice. "Besides, I don't care what anyone thinks, I love you too much."

"Oh, Kitty, I don't deserve you!" he groaned before he kissed her again. Kitty moaned a little against his eager mouth as his hands caressed her back, and his arms held her close. She was a most willing captive.

Sometime later, he raised his head an inch or so and whispered, "So, you will consent to play cat to my lion, will you, Kitty?"

Lady Catherine Cahill leaned back against those strong arms and smiled up at him, her head on one side as she regarded his smiling eyes, his contented expression. Then, sighing again, she put her face against his stiff shirt front. As her arms came around his waist, Lionel Eden, Viscount Benning, heard the sound she was making deep in her throat against his rib cage, and he put back his head and laughed in pure delight.

For the Lady Catherine Cahill was purring.

About the Author

Although Barbara Hazard is a New England Yankee by birth, upbringing, and education, she is of English descent on both sides of her family and has many relatives in that country. The Regency period has always been a favorite, and when she began to write nine years ago, she gravitated to it naturally, feeling perfectly at home there. Barbara Hazard now lives in New York. She has been a musician and an artist, and although writing is her first love, she also enjoys classical music, reading, and quilting.